KITCHEN

KITCHEN

BANANA YOSHIMOTO

Translated from the Japanese by Megan Backus

GROVE PRESS   NEW YORK

KITCHEN by Banana Yoshimoto

Copyright © 1988 by Banana Yoshimoto. English translation rights arranged with Fukutake Publishing Co., Ltd., through the Japan Foreign-Rights Centre.

Translation copyright © 1993 by Megan Backus

Published by Grove Press
A division of Grove Press, Inc.
841 Broadway
New York, NY 10003–4793

Published in Canada by General Publishing Company, Inc.

Library of Congress Cataloging-in-Publication Data

Yoshimoto, Banana, 1964–
   [Kitchin. English]
   Kitchen / Banana Yoshimoto.
     p.   cm.
   Translation of: Kitchin.
   ISBN 0–8021–1516–0
   I. Title.
  PL865.07138K5813   1993
  895.6'35—dc20   92-12871
                                            CIP

Manufactured in the United States of America
Printed on acid-free paper
First English-language edition 1993

10 9 8 7 6 5 4 3 2 1

CONTENTS

KITCHEN

me - KAH - gay
eh - REE - ko
you - EE - chi
you - bEE
So - TAH - ro
Sen - SAY

1 KITCHEN

The place I like best in this world is the kitchen. No matter where it is, no matter what kind, if it's a kitchen, if it's a place where they make food, it's fine with me. Ideally it should be well broken in. Lots of tea towels, dry and immaculate. White tile catching the light (ting! ting!).

I love even incredibly dirty kitchens to distraction—vegetable droppings all over the floor, so dirty your slippers turn black on the bottom. Strangely, it's better if this kind of kitchen is large. I lean up against the silver door of a towering, giant refrigerator stocked with enough food to get through a winter. When I raise my eyes from the oil-spattered gas burner and the rusty kitchen knife, outside the window stars are glittering, lonely.

Now only the kitchen and I are left. It's just a little nicer than being all alone.

When I'm dead worn out, in a reverie, I often think that when it comes time to die, I want to breathe my last in a kitchen. Whether it's cold and I'm all alone, or somebody's there and it's warm, I'll stare death fearlessly in the eye. If it's a kitchen, I'll think, "How good."

Before the Tanabe family took me in, I spent every night in the kitchen. After my grandmother died, I couldn't sleep. One morning at dawn I trundled out of my room in search of comfort and found that the one place I *could* sleep was beside the refrigerator.

My parents—my name is Mikage Sakurai—both died when they were young. After that my grandparents brought me up. I was going into junior high when my grandfather died. From then on, it was just my grandmother and me.

When my grandmother died the other day, I was taken by surprise. My family had steadily decreased one by one as the years went by, but when it suddenly dawned on me that I was all alone, everything before my eyes seemed false. The fact that time continued to pass in the usual way in this apartment where I grew up, even though now I was here all alone, amazed me. It was total science fiction. The blackness of the cosmos.

Three days after the funeral I was still in a daze. Steeped in a sadness so great I could barely cry, shuffling softly in gentle drowsiness, I pulled my futon into the deathly silent, gleaming kitchen. Wrapped in a blanket, like Linus, I slept. The hum of the refrigerator kept me from thinking of my loneliness. There, the long night came on in perfect peace, and morning came.

But . . . I just wanted to sleep under the stars.

I wanted to wake up in the morning light.

Aside from that, I just drifted, listless.

However! I couldn't exist like that. Reality is wonderful.

I thought of the money my grandmother had left me— just enough. The place was too big, too expensive, for one person. I had to look for another apartment. There was no way around it. I thumbed through the listings, but when I saw so many places all the same lined up like that, it made my head swim. Moving takes a lot of time and trouble. It takes energy.

I had no strength; my joints ached from sleeping in the kitchen day and night. When I realized how much effort moving would require—I'd have to pull myself together and go look at places. Move my stuff. Get a phone installed—I lay around instead, sleeping, in despair. It was then that a miracle, a godsend, came calling one afternoon. I remember it well.

Dingdong. Suddenly the doorbell rang.

It was a somewhat cloudy spring afternoon. I was intently involved in tying up old magazines with string while glancing at the apartment listings with half an eye but no interest, wondering how I was going to move. Flustered, looking like I'd just gotten out of bed, I ran out and without thinking undid the latch and opened the door. Thank god it wasn't a robber. There stood Yuichi Tanabe.

"Thank you for your help the other day," I said. He was a nice young man, a year younger than me, who had helped out a lot at the funeral. I think he'd said he went to the same university I did. I was taking time off.

"Not at all," he said. "Did you decide on a place to live yet?"

"Not even close." I smiled.

"I see."

"Would you like to come in for some tea?"

"No. I'm on my way somewhere and I'm kind of in a hurry." He grinned. "I just stopped by to ask you something. I was talking to my mother, and we were thinking you ought to come to our house for a while."

"Huh?" I said.

"In any case, why don't you come over tonight around seven? Here's the directions."

"Okay . . ." I said vacantly, taking the slip of paper.

"All right, then, good. Mom and I are both looking forward to your coming." His smile was so bright as he stood in my doorway that I zoomed in for a closeup on his pupils. I couldn't take my eyes off him. I think I heard a spirit call my name.

"Okay," I said. "I'll be there."

Bad as it sounds, it was like I was possessed. His attitude was so totally "cool," though, I felt I could trust him. In the black gloom before my eyes (as it always is in cases of bewitchment), I saw a straight road leading from me to him. He seemed to glow with white light. That was the effect he had on me.

"Okay, see you later," he said, smiling, and left.

Before my grandmother's funeral I had barely known him. On the day itself, when Yuichi Tanabe showed up all of a sudden, I actually wondered if he had been her lover. His hands trembled as he lit the incense; his eyes were swollen from crying. When he saw my grandmother's picture on the altar, again his tears fell like rain. My first thought when I saw that was that my love for my own grandmother was nothing compared to this boy's, whoever he was. He looked that sad.

Then, mopping his face with a handkerchief, he said, "Let me help with something." After that, he helped me a lot.

Yuichi Tanabe . . . I must have been quite confused if I took that long to remember when I'd heard grandmother mention his name.

He was the boy who worked part-time at my grandmother's favorite flower shop. I remembered hearing her say, any number of times, things like, "What a nice boy they have working there. . . . That Tanabe boy . . . today, again . . ." Grandmother loved cut flowers. Because the ones in our kitchen were not allowed to wilt, she'd go to the flower shop a couple of times a week. When I thought of that, I remembered him walking behind my grandmother, a large potted plant in his arms.

He was a long-limbed young man with pretty features. I didn't know anything more about him, but I might have seen him hard at work in the flower shop. Even after I got to know him a little I still had an impression of aloofness. No matter how nice his manner and expression, he seemed like a loner. I barely knew him, really.

It was raining that hazy spring night. A gentle, warm rain enveloped the neighborhood as I walked with directions in hand.

My apartment building and the one where the Tanabes lived were separated by Chuo Park. As I crossed through, I was inundated with the green smell of the night. I walked, sloshing down the shiny wet path that glittered with the colors of the rainbow.

To be frank, I was only going because they'd asked me. I didn't think about it beyond that. I looked up at the towering apartment building and thought, their apartment on the tenth floor is so high, the view must be beautiful at night. . . .

Getting off the elevator, I was alarmed by the sound of my own footsteps in the hall. I rang the bell, and abruptly, Yuichi opened the door. "Come in."

"Thanks." I stepped inside. The room was truly strange.

First thing, as I looked toward the kitchen, my gaze landed with a thud on the enormous sofa in the living room. Against the backdrop of the large kitchen with its shelves of pots and pans—no table, no carpet, just "it."

Covered in beige fabric, it looked like something out of a commercial. An entire family could watch TV on it. A dog too big to keep in Japan could stretch out across it—sideways. It was really a marvelous sofa.

In front of the large window leading onto the terrace was a jungle of plants growing in bowls, planters, and all kinds of pots. Looking around, I saw that the whole house was filled with flowers; there were vases full of spring blooms everywhere.

"My mother says she'll get away from work soon. Take a look around if you'd like. Should I give you the tour? Or pick a room, then I'll know what kind of person you are," said Yuichi, making tea.

"What kind? . . ." I seated myself on the deep, comfy sofa.

"I mean, what you want to know about a house and the people who live there, their tastes. A lot of people would say you learn a lot from the toilet," he said, smiling, unconcerned. He had a very relaxed way of talking.

"The kitchen," I said.

"Well, here it is. Look at whatever you want."

While he made tea, I explored the kitchen. I took everything in: the good quality of the mat on the wood floor and of Yuichi's slippers; a practical minimum of well-worn kitchen things, precisely arranged. A Silverstone frying pan and a delightful German-made vegetable peeler—a peeler to make even the laziest grandmother enjoy slip, slipping those skins off.

Lit by a small fluorescent lamp, all kinds of plates silently awaited their turns; glasses sparkled. It was clear that in

9

spite of the disorder everything was of the finest quality. There were things with special uses, like . . . porcelain bowls, *gratin* dishes, gigantic platters, two beer steins. Somehow it was all very satisfying. I even opened the small refrigerator (Yuichi said it was okay)—everything was neatly organized, nothing just "left."

I looked around, nodding and murmuring approvingly, "Mmm, mmm." It was a good kitchen. I fell in love with it at first sight.

I went back and sat on the sofa, and out came hot tea.

Usually, the first time I go to a house, face to face with people I barely know, I feel an immense loneliness. I saw myself reflected in the glass of the large terrace window while black gloom spread over the rain-hounded night panorama. I was tied by blood to no creature in this world. I could go anywhere, do anything. It was dizzying.

Suddenly, to see that the world was so large, the cosmos so black. The unbounded fascination of it, the unbounded loneliness . . . For the first time, these days, I was touching it with these hands, these eyes. I've been looking at the world half-blind, I thought.

"Why did you invite me here?" I asked.

"We thought you might be having a hard time," Yuichi said, peering kindly at me. "Your grandmother was always so sweet to me, and look at this house, we have all this room. Shouldn't you be moving?"

"Yes. Although the landlord's been nice enough to give me extra time."

"So why not move in with us?" he said, as though it were the most natural thing in the world.

He struck just the right note, neither cold nor oppressively kind. It made me warm to him; my heart welled up to the point of tears. Just then, with the scratch of a key in the door, an incredibly beautiful woman came running in, all out of breath.

I was so stunned, I gaped. Though she didn't seem young, she was truly beautiful. From her outfit and dramatic makeup, which really wouldn't do for daytime, I understood that hers was night work.

Yuichi introduced me: "This is Mikage Sakurai."

"How do you do," she said in a slightly husky voice, still panting, with a smile. "I'm Yuichi's mother. My name is Eriko."

This was his mother? Dumbfounded, I couldn't take my eyes off her. Hair that rustled like silk to her shoulders; the deep sparkle of her long, narrow eyes; well-formed lips, a nose with a high, straight bridge—the whole of her gave off a marvelous light that seemed to vibrate with life force. She didn't look human. I had never seen anyone like her.

I was staring to the point of rudeness. "How do you do," I replied at last, smiling back at her.

"We're so pleased to have you here," she said to me warmly, and then, turning to Yuichi, "I'm sorry, Yuichi. I just can't get away tonight. I dashed out for a second saying that I was off to the bathroom. But I'll have plenty of time in the morning. I hope Mikage will agree to spend the night." She was in a rush and ran to the door, red dress flying.

"I'll drive you," said Yuichi.

"Sorry to put you to so much trouble," I said.

"Not at all. Who ever would have thought the club would be so busy tonight? It's me who should apologize. Well! See you in the morning!"

She ran out in her high heels, and Yuichi called back to me, "Wait here! Watch TV or something!" then ran after her, leaving me alone in a daze.

I felt certain that if you looked really closely you would see a few normal signs of age—crow's feet, less-than-perfect teeth—some part of her that looked like a real human being. Still, she was stunning. She made me want to be with her again. There was a warm light, like her afterimage, softly glowing in my heart. That must be what they mean by "charm." Like Helen Keller when she understood "water" for the first time, the word burst into reality for me, its living example before my eyes. It's no exaggeration; the encounter was that overwhelming.

Yuichi returned, jingling the car keys. "If she could only get away for ten minutes, she should have just called," he said, taking off his shoes in the entryway.

I stayed where I was on the sofa and answered "Mmm," noncommittally.

"Mikage," he said, "were you a little bit intimidated by my mother?"

"Yes," I told him frankly. "I've never seen a woman that beautiful."

"Yes. But . . ." Smiling, he sat down on the floor

right in front of me. "She's had plastic surgery."

"Oh?" I said, feigning nonchalance. "I wondered why she didn't look anything like you."

"And that's not all. Guess what else—she's a man." He could barely contain his amusement.

This was too much. I just stared at him in wide-eyed silence. I expected any second he would say, "Just kidding." Those tapered fingers, those mannerisms, the way she carried herself . . . I held my breath remembering that beautiful face; he, on the other hand, was enjoying this.

"Yes, but . . ." My mouth hung open. "You've been saying all along, 'my mother' this, and 'my mother' that. . . ."

"Yes, but. Could *you* call someone who looked like that 'Dad'?" he asked calmly. He has a point, I thought. An extremely good answer.

"What about the name Eriko?"

"It's actually Yuji."

It was as though there were a haze in front of my eyes. When I was finally ready to hear the story, I said, "So, who gave birth to you?"

"Eriko was a man a long time ago. He married very young. The person he married was my mother."

"Wow . . . I wonder what she was like." I couldn't imagine.

"I don't remember her myself. She died when I was little. I have a picture, though. Want to see it?"

"Yes." I nodded. Without getting up, he dragged his bag across the floor, then took an old photograph out of his wallet and handed it to me.

She was someone whose face told you nothing about

13

her. Short hair, small eyes and nose. The impression was of a very odd woman of indeterminate age. When I didn't say anything, Yuichi said, "She looks strange, doesn't she?"

I smiled uncomfortably.

"As a child Eriko was taken in by her family. I don't know why. They grew up together. Even as a man he was good-looking, and apparently he was very popular with women. Why he would marry such a strange . . ." he said smiling, looking at the photo. "He must have been pretty attached to my mother. So much so he turned his back on the debt of gratitude he owed his foster parents and eloped with her."

I nodded.

"After my real mother died, Eriko quit her job, gathered me up, and asked herself, 'What do I want to do now?' What she decided was, 'Become a woman.' She knew she'd never love anybody else. She says that before she became a woman she was very shy. Because she hates to do things halfway, she had everything 'done,' from her face to her whatever, and with the money she had left over she bought that nightclub. She raised me a woman alone, as it were." He smiled.

"What an *amazing* life story!"

"She's not dead yet," said Yuichi.

Whether I could trust him or whether he still had something up his sleeve . . . the more I found out about these people, the more I didn't know what to expect.

But I trusted their kitchen. Even though they didn't

look alike, there were certain traits they shared. Their faces shone like buddhas when they smiled. I like that, I thought.

"I'll be out of here early in the morning, so just help yourself to whatever you want."

A sleepy-looking Yuichi, his arms full of blankets, pillows, and pajamas for me, showed me how the shower worked and pointed out the towels.

Unable to think of much of anything after hearing such a (fantastic!) life story, I had watched a video with Yuichi. We had chatted about things like the flower shop and my grandmother, and time passed quickly. Now it was one in the morning. That sofa was delectable. It was so big, so soft, so deep, I felt that once I surrendered to it I'd never get up again.

"Your mother," I said after a while. "I bet the first time she sat on this sofa in the furniture store, she just had to have it and bought it right then and there."

"You got it," he said. "As soon as she gets an idea in her head she does it, you know? I just stand back in amazement at her way of making things happen."

"No kidding."

"So that sofa is yours for the time being. It's your bed. It's great for us to be able to put it to good use."

"Is it," I ventured softly, "is it really okay for me to sleep here?"

"Sure," he said, without a hint of hesitation.

"I'm very grateful."

After the usual instructions on how to make myself at home, he said good night and went to his room.

I was sleepy, too.

Showering at someone else's house, I thought about what was happening to me, and my exhaustions washed away under the hot water.

I put on the borrowed pajamas and, barefoot, went into the silent living room. I just had to go back for one more look at the kitchen. It was really a good kitchen.

Then I stumbled over to the sofa that was to be my bed for the night and turned out the lamp. Suspended in the dim light before the window overlooking the magnificent tenth-floor view, the plants breathed softly, resting. By now the rain had stopped, and the atmosphere, sparkling, replete with moisture, refracted the glittering night splendidly.

Wrapped in blankets, I thought how funny it was that tonight, too, here I was sleeping next to the kitchen. I smiled to myself. But this time I wasn't lonely. Maybe I had been waiting for this. Maybe all I had been hoping for was a bed in which to be able to stop thinking, just for a little while, about what happened before and what would happen in the future. I was too sad to be able to sleep in the same bed with anyone; that would only make the sadness worse. But here was a kitchen, some plants, someone sleeping in the next room, perfect quiet . . . this was the best. This place was . . . the best.

At peace, I slept.

★   ★   ★

I awoke to the sound of running water.

Morning had come, dazzling. I arose drowsily and went into the kitchen. There was "Eriko-san," her back turned to me. Her clothing was subdued compared to last night's, but as she turned to me with a cheery "Good morning!" her face, even more brilliantly animated, brought me to my senses. "Good morning," I answered. She opened the refrigerator, glanced inside, and looked at me with a troubled air.

"You know," she said, "I'm always hungry in the morning, even though I'm still sleepy. But there's nothing to eat in this house. Let's call for takeout. What would you like?"

I stood up. "Would you like me to make something?"

"Really?" she said, and then, doubtfully, "Do you think you can handle a knife, half-asleep?"

"No problem."

The entire apartment was filled with light, like a sunroom. I looked out at the sweet, endless blue of the sky; it was glorious.

In the joy of being in a kitchen I liked so well, my head cleared, and suddenly I remembered she was a man. I turned to look at her. Déjà vu overwhelmed me like a flash flood.

The house smelled of wood. I felt an immense nostalgia, in that downpour of morning light, watching her pull a cushion onto the floor in that dusty living room and curl up to watch TV.

* * *

She attacked the food—cucumber salad and soupy rice with eggs—with gusto.

It was midday. From the building's garden we could hear the shouts of children playing in the springlike weather. The plants near the window, enveloped in the gentle sunlight, sparkled bright green; far off in the pale sky, thin clouds gently flowed, suspended. It was a warm, lazy afternoon.

I couldn't have dreamed of this yesterday morning, this scene of having breakfast at the house of someone I had just met, and it felt very strange. There we were, eating breakfast, all sorts of things set out directly on the floor (there was no table). The sunlight shone through our cups, and our cold green tea reflected prettily against the floor.

Suddenly Eriko looked me full in the face. "Yuichi told me before that you reminded him of Woofie, a dog we used to have. And you know—it's really true."

"His name was Woofie?"

"Yes, or Wolfie."

"Hmm," I said, thinking, "Woofie."

"You have the same nice eyes, the same nice hair. . . . When I saw you for the first time yesterday, I had to force myself not to laugh. You really do look like him."

"Is that right?" Not that I believed I looked like a dog, but I thought, if Woofie was a Saint Bernard, that would be pretty awful.

"When Woofie died I couldn't get Yuichi to eat a bite, not a grain of rice, nothing. So it follows that Yuichi feels close to you. I can't guarantee it's romantic, though!" Mom shook with laughter.

"Okay," I said.

"Yuichi says your grandmother was very kind."

"Grandmother was really fond of him."

"That boy. You know, I haven't been able to devote myself full-time to raising him, and I'm afraid there are some things that slipped through the cracks."

I smiled. "Slipped through the cracks?"

"It's true," she said with a motherly smile. "He's confused about emotional things and he's strangely distant with people. I know I haven't done everything right. . . . But I wanted above all to make a good kid out of him and I focused everything on raising him that way. And you know, he is. A good kid."

"I know."

"You're a good kid, too." She beamed.

Her power was the brilliance of her charm and it had brought her to where she was now. I had the feeling that neither her wife nor her son could diminish it. That quality must have condemned her to an ice-cold loneliness.

She said, munching cucumbers, "You know, a lot of people say things they don't mean. But I'm serious: I want you to stay here as long as you like. You're a good kid, and having you here makes me truly happy. I understand what it's like to be hurt and to have nowhere to go. Please, stay with us and don't worry about anything. Okay?"

She emphasized her words by looking deep into my eyes.

". . . Naturally, I'll pay rent and everything," I said,

desperately moved. My chest was full to bursting. "But yes, till I find another place to live, I'd really appreciate your putting me up."

"Of course, of course, think nothing of it. But instead of rent, just make us soupy rice once in a while. Yours is so much better than Yuichi's," she said, smiling.

To live alone with an old person is terribly nerve-racking, and the healthier he or she is, the more one worries. Actually, when I lived with my grandmother this didn't occur to me; I enjoyed it. But looking back, I can't help thinking that deep down I was always, at all times, afraid: "Grandma's going to die."

When I came home, my grandmother would come out of the Japanese-style room where the TV was and say, "Welcome home." If I came in late I always brought her sweets. She was a pretty relaxed grandmother and never gave me a hard time if I told her I was going to sleep over somewhere or whatever. We would spend a little time together before bed, sometimes drinking coffee, sometimes green tea, eating cake and watching TV.

In my grandmother's room, which hadn't changed since I was little, we would tell each other silly gossip, talk about TV stars or what had happened that day; we talked about whatever. I think she even told me about Yuichi during those times.

No matter how dreamlike a love I have found myself in, no matter how delightfully drunk I have been, in my heart

I was always aware that my family consisted of only one other person.

The space that cannot be filled, no matter how cheerfully a child and an old person are living together—the deathly silence that, panting in a corner of the room, pushes its way in like a shudder. I felt it very early, although no one told me about it.

I think Yuichi did, too.

When was it I realized that, on this truly dark and solitary path we all walk, the only way we can light is our own? Although I was raised with love, I was always lonely.

Someday, without fail, everyone will disappear, scattered into the blackness of time. I've always lived with that knowledge rooted in my being: perhaps that's why Yuichi's way of reacting to things seemed natural to me.

And that's why I rushed into living with them.

I gave myself permission to be lazy until May. I was in paradise. I still went to my part-time job, but after that I would clean house, watch TV, bake cakes: I lived like a housewife.

Little by little, light and air came into my heart. I was thrilled.

What with Yuichi's school and job, and Eriko's working at night, the three of us were almost never home at the same time. At first I would get tired. I wasn't used to sleeping in the living room, and I was constantly coming and going between the Tanabes' and the old apartment to get things in order, but I soon got used to it.

I loved the Tanabes' sofa as much as I loved their kitchen. I came to crave sleeping on it. Listening to the quiet breathing of the plants, sensing the night view through the curtains, I slept like a baby. There wasn't anything more I wanted. I was happy.

I've always been like that—if I'm not pushed to the brink, I won't move. This time it was the same. For having been granted such a warm bed after finding myself in the direst straits, I thanked the gods—whether they existed or not—with all my heart.

One day I went back to the old apartment to take care of the last of my things. When I opened the door, I shuddered. It was like coming back to a stranger's house.

Cold and dark, not a sigh to be heard. Everything there, which should have been so familiar, seemed to be turning away from me. I entered gingerly, on tiptoe, feeling as though I should ask permission.

When my grandmother died, time died, too, in this apartment. The reality of that fact was immediate. There was nothing I could do to change it. Other than turning around and leaving, there was only one thing to do— humming a tune, I began to scrub the refrigerator.

Just then the telephone rang.

I picked up the receiver, knowing who it would be. It was Sotaro. He was my old . . . boyfriend. We broke up about the time my grandmother's illness got bad.

"Hello? Mikage?" The sound of his voice made me want to weep with nostalgia.

"Long time no see!" I cried out joyfully. We were beyond displays of shyness.

"Yeah, well, you haven't been coming to classes, so I started wondering what was wrong and I asked around. They told me your grandmother had died. I was shocked. . . . That's really rough."

"Yes. So I've been pretty busy."

"Can you come out now?"

"Sure."

As we decided where to meet, I looked up at the window. The sky outside was a dull gray. Waves of clouds were being pushed around by the wind with amazing force. In this world there is no place for sadness. No place; not one.

Sotaro loved parks.

Green places, open spaces, the outdoors—he loved all of that, and at school he was often to be found in the middle of a garden or sitting on a bench beside a playground. The fact that if you wanted to find Sotaro you'd find him amid greenery had entered into university lore. He was planning to do some kind of work with plants.

For some reason I keep getting connected to men who have something to do with plants.

We were the very picture of a student couple in my happier days (Sotaro is always cheerful). Because of his obsession we would plan to meet outside even in the middle of winter, but I was late so often that we found a compromise meeting place. We hit on a ridiculously large coffee shop on the edge of the park.

So this day, too, there was Sotaro, sitting in the seat nearest the park in that large coffee shop, looking out the window. Outside, against the backdrop of the entirely overcast sky, the trees trembled in the wind, rustling. I made my way over to him, snaking around the comings and goings of the waitresses. He smiled when he saw me.

I sat down across from him and said, "I wonder if it's going to rain."

"Naah, it's clearing up, don't you think? Funny, isn't it, we haven't seen each other in all this time and we talk about the weather." His smiling face put me at ease.

It's so great, I thought, having tea in the afternoon with someone you really feel at home with. I knew how wildly he tosses in his sleep, how much milk and sugar he takes in his coffee. I knew his face in front of the mirror, insanely serious, as he tries to tame his mop of unruly hair with the hair dryer. Then I thought, if we were still together I would be worrying about how I've just chipped the nail polish on my right hand scrubbing the refrigerator.

In the middle of gossipy chitchat, as if suddenly remembering something, he changed the subject. "I hear you're living with that Tanabe guy."

That startled me. I was so surprised I let my cup tilt sideways and spilled my tea into the saucer.

"It's the talk of the school. Don't tell me you hadn't heard?" he said, looking upset but still smiling.

"I just didn't know that you knew. What happened?"

"Tanabe's girlfriend—or should I say former girl-friend?—anyway, she slapped him. In the cafeteria."

"What? Because of me?"

"Seems that way. But you two must be pretty cozy. That's what I hear, anyway."

"Really? It's the first I've heard of it," I said.

"But you're living with him, aren't you?"

"His mother lives there too!" (All right, "mother" wasn't strictly correct, but . . .)

"What?! Don't lie to me!" Sotaro said in a loud voice. In the old days I loved him for his lively frankness, but right now it struck me as obnoxious, and I was only mortified.

"This Tanabe guy," he said, "I hear he's pretty weird."

"I wouldn't know," I said. "I hardly ever see him . . . and we don't talk much. They just took me in like they would a dog. It's not that he especially likes me or any-thing. So I don't know anything about him. And I had no idea about that stupid incident."

"It's just that I often don't understand who you like, or love, or whatever," said Sotaro. "In any case it seems like a good thing for you. How long are you going to stay there?"

"I don't know."

"Well, hadn't you better decide?" he said, laughing.

"I intend to," I answered.

On the way home we walked through the park. There was a good view of the Tanabes' building through the trees.

"That's where I live," I said, pointing it out.

"How great—right next to the park. If I lived there I'd get up every morning at five and take a walk." Sotaro smiled. He was very tall, and I was always looking up at him. Glancing at his profile, I thought, if I were with him, he would . . . he would grab me by the hair, force me to decide on an apartment, and pull me kicking and screaming back to school.

I loved his hearty robustness, I thirsted after it, but in spite of that I couldn't keep pace with it, and it made me hate myself. In the old days.

He was the eldest son of a large family; without being aware of it he got his sunny outlook from them, and I had been drawn to it. But what I needed now was the Tanabes' strange cheerfulness, their tranquility, and I didn't even consider trying to explain that to him. It wasn't especially necessary, and I knew it would be impossible anyway. When I got together with Sotaro, it was always like that. Just being myself made me terribly sad.

"Well, bye."

From deep in my heart, my eyes asked the question: Before it's too late, do you still feel anything for me?

"Chin up, kid!" He smiled, but the answer was clear in his own eyes.

"Okay," I said, and waving, we parted. The feeling traveled to some infinitely distant place and disappeared.

That evening, as I was watching a video, the door opened and there was Yuichi, a large box in his arms.

"You're home," I said.

"I bought a word processor," Yuichi exclaimed happily. It had begun to occur to me: these people had a taste for buying new things that verged on the unhealthy. And I mean big purchases. Mainly electronic stuff.

"That's great."

"Anything you need to have typed?"

"Yes, come to think of it." I was thinking, maybe I'll have him type up some song lyrics or something, when he said, "Right. Shouldn't you be sending out change-of-address cards?"

"What are you talking about?"

"Well, how long do you intend to go on living in this huge city without an address or phone number?"

"But it seems like a lot of trouble, considering I'm going to move and I'd have to do it all again."

"Fuck that!" he burst out, and then, softening, "Okay, just please do it."

But what I had heard from Sotaro was still fresh in my mind. "Yes, but don't you think it's a little weird, my living here? Doesn't it cause problems for you?"

"What are you talking about?" he said, giving me a mystified, stupid look. Had he been my boyfriend, I would have wanted to slap him. My own dependent position aside, for a moment I hated him. How dense could he be?

I have recently moved. Please reach me at the following address and telephone number:

Mikage Sakurai
tel. XXX-XXXX
XX Apartments, No. 1002
XX Ward, XX 3–21–1
Tokyo

Yuichi gave me the above as a model, then, while running out copies (I should have known these people would have a photocopier stashed away), I began addressing envelopes. Yuichi helped me; he seemed to have some spare time tonight. Something else I realized was that he hated spare time.

The scratching of our pens mingled with the sound of raindrops beginning to fall in the transparent stillness of the evening.

Outside, a warm wind came roaring up, a spring storm. It seemed to shake the very night view out the terrace window. I continued down the list of my friends' names, quietly nostalgic. I accidentally skipped Sotaro. The wind was . . . strong. We could hear the trees and telephone lines rattling. I closed my eyes, my elbows resting on the small folding table, and my thoughts skittered out to the row of shops along the now-silent street below. What was this table doing in the apartment? I couldn't know. She about whom Yuichi had said, "As soon as she gets an idea in her head, she does it, you know?" must have bought it.

"Don't fall asleep," said Yuichi.

"I'm not. I really love doing this, writing change-of-address cards."

"Yeah, me too. Moving, writing postcards on trips, I really love it."

"Yeah, but . . ." I broached the subject a second time. "These postcards are going to make waves. Won't you get slapped in the school cafeteria?"

"Is that what you heard today?" He smiled bitterly. It gave me a start in its contrast to his usual smile.

"Well then, isn't it better to just be honest about it? You've done plenty for me already."

"Cut the crap," he said. "You think this is the postcard game we're playing here?"

"What's 'the postcard game'?"

"I don't know . . ."

We laughed. After that, somehow the conversation strayed off the subject. Even I, slow as I am, finally understood his excessive unnaturalness. When I took a good look in his eyes, I understood.

He was terribly, terribly sad.

Sotaro had said that even though she'd been seeing him for a year, Yuichi's girlfriend didn't understand the slightest thing about him, and it made her angry. She said Yuichi was incapable of caring more for a girl than he did for a fountain pen.

Because I wasn't in love with Yuichi, I understood that very well. The quality and importance of a fountain pen meant to him something completely different from what it meant to her. Perhaps there are people in this world who love their fountain pens with every fiber of their being— and that's very sad. If you're not in love with him, you can understand him.

"It couldn't be helped," said Yuichi without raising his head. He seemed bothered by my silence. "It was in no way your fault."

"Thanks." For some reason *I* was thanking *him*.

"You're welcome," he said, laughing.

I've touched him, I thought. After a month of living in the same place, at close quarters, I've touched him for the first time. In that case, I might end up falling in love with him. When I've fallen in love before, I've always tried to run it down and tackle it, but with him it would be different. The conversation we just had was like a glimpse of stars through a chink in a cloudy sky—perhaps, over time, talks like this would lead to love.

But—I was thinking while I wrote—I must move out.

It was patently obvious that the trouble between Yuichi and his girlfriend was my living here. As to how strong I was, or whether I would soon be ready to go back to living alone, I couldn't venture a guess. Still, I told myself, soon, of course, very soon—although telling myself this while writing my change-of-address cards could be considered a contradiction.

I had to move out.

Just then the door opened with a squeal of hinges, and in came Eriko holding a large paper bag. I looked at her in surprise.

"What's going on? What's happening at the club?" said Yuichi, turning around to face her.

"I'm going right after this. Listen, guess what I bought: a juicer," said Eriko happily, pulling a large box from the paper bag. Unbelievable, these people, I thought. "I just came home to drop it off. Go ahead, use it."

"If you'd called, I would have gone and picked it up." Yuichi was already cutting the string with scissors.

"It's no trouble, it wasn't heavy."

In short order the package was open, and a magnificent juicer that seemed able to make any kind of juice was drawn out of it.

"I hear fresh-squeezed juice gives you beautiful skin," said Eriko, delighted.

"It's a little late for that at your age," retorted Yuichi, not raising his eyes from the instruction booklet.

The incredible ease and nonchalance of the conversation made my brain reel. It was like watching *Bewitched*. That they could be this cheerfully normal in the midst of such extreme abnormality.

"Oh!" cried Eriko. "Is Mikage writing her change-of-address cards? This is perfect. I have a moving-in gift for her."

Then she produced another package, this one wrapped round and round with paper. When I opened it, I saw that it was a pretty glass decorated with a banana motif.

"Be sure to drink lots of juice, okay?" said Eriko.

"Maybe we should drink banana juice," said Yuichi with a straight face.

"Wow!" I said, on the verge of tears. "I'm so happy!"

When I move out I'll take this glass with me, and even after I move out I'll come back again and again to make soupy rice for you. I was thinking that but wasn't able to say it. What a special, special glass!

The next day was when I had to clear out of the old apartment for good; at last I got it cleaned out completely. I was feeling very sluggish. It was a clear, bright afternoon, windless and cloudless, and a warm, golden sunlight filled the empty rooms I had once called home.

By way of apology for taking so much time, I went to visit the landlord.

Like we often did when I was a child, we drank tea and chatted in his office. I felt very keenly how old he had become. Just as my grandmother had often sat here, now I was in the same little chair, drinking tea and talking about the weather and the state of the neighborhood. It was strange; it didn't seem right.

An irresistible shift had put the past behind me. I had recoiled in a daze; all I could do was react weakly. But it was not I who was doing the shifting—on the contrary. For me everything had been agony.

Until only recently, the light that bathed the now-empty apartment had contained the smells of our life there.

The kitchen window. The smiling faces of friends, the fresh greenery of the university campus as a backdrop to Sotaro's profile, my grandmother's voice on the phone when I called her late at night, my warm bed on cold mornings, the sound of my grandmother's slippers in the hallway, the color of the curtains . . . the *tatami* mat . . . the clock on the wall.

All of it. Everything that was no longer there.

When I left the apartment it was already evening.

Pale twilight was descending. The wind was coming up,

a little chilly on the skin. I waited for the bus, the hem of my thin coat fluttering in the gusts.

I watched the rows of windows in the tall building across the street from the bus stop, suspended, emitting a pretty blue light. The people moving behind those windows, the elevators going up and down, all of it, sparkling silently, seemed to melt into the half-darkness.

I carried the last of my things in both hands. When I thought, now at last I won't be torn between two places, I began to feel strangely shaky, close to tears.

The bus appeared around the corner. It seemed to float to a stop before my eyes, and the people lined up, got on, one by one.

It was packed. I stood, with my hand on the crowded strap, watching the darkening sky disappear beyond the distant buildings.

When the bus took off my eye came to rest on the still-new moon making its gentle way across the sky.

My angry, irritable reaction to the jarring each time the bus lurched to a stop told me how tired I was. Again and again, with each angry stop, I would look outside and watch a dirigible drifting across the far-off sky. Propelled by the wind, it slowly moved along.

Staring at it intently, I felt happy. The dirigible traversed the sky like a pale moonbeam, its tiny lights blinking on and off.

Then an old lady sitting beside her little granddaughter, who was directly in front of me, said in a low voice, "Look, Yuki, a dirigible. Look! Look! Isn't it beautiful?"

The little girl, whose face epitomized "grandchild," was in a very bad mood, perhaps because of the traffic jam and crowdedness. She said angrily, fidgeting, "I don't care. And it's not a dirigible!"

"Maybe you're right," said the grandmother, smiling brightly, not at all annoyed.

Yuki continued her whiny pouting. "Aren't we there yet? I'm sleepy."

The brat! I, too, had acted that way when I was tired. You'll regret it, I thought, talking to your grandmother that way.

"Don't worry, we'll be there soon. Look, look behind you. Mommy's asleep. You don't want to wake her, do you, Yuki?"

"Oh! She is, isn't she?" Turning around to look at her sleeping mother in the back of the bus, Yuki finally smiled.

Isn't that nice, I thought. Hearing the grandmother's gentle words and seeing the child's face suddenly turn adorable when she smiled, I became envious. I'd never see my own grandmother again.

Never again. I don't care for the loaded sentimentality of those words or for the feeling of limitation they impose. But just then they struck me with an unforgettable intensity and authority. I intended to think them over dispassionately. Jostled by the motion of the bus, I was determined to keep that dirigible, so far off in the sky, in sight no matter what. But then, overpowered by their enormous weight, I found that tears were pouring down my cheeks and onto my blouse.

I was surprised. Am I losing my mind? I wondered. It was like being falling-down drunk: my body was independent of me. Before I knew it, tears were flooding out. I felt myself turning bright red with embarrassment and got off the bus. I watched it drive away, and then without thinking I ducked into a poorly lit alley.

Jammed between my own bags, stooped over, I sobbed. I had never cried this way in my life. As the hot tears poured out, I remembered that I had never had a proper cry over my grandmother's death. I had a feeling that I wasn't crying over any one sad thing, but rather for many.

Looking up, I saw white steam rising, in the dark, out of a brightly lit window overhead. I listened. From inside came the sound of happy voices at work, soup boiling, knives and pots and pans clanging.

It was a kitchen.

I was puzzled, smiling about how I had just gone from the darkest despair to feeling wonderful. I stood up, smoothed down my skirt, and started back for the Tanabes'.

I implored the gods: Please, let me live.

"I'm sleepy," I announced to Yuichi, and went straight to bed. It had been a prodigiously tiring day. But still, unburdened after my good cry, I slept like a baby.

I had a feeling that I heard, in some part of my brain, Yuichi going into the kitchen for tea and saying, "What? Are you really already asleep?"

★   ★   ★

I had a dream.

I was scrubbing the sink in the kitchen of the apartment I had cleared out of that day. Funny, but what made me feel most nostalgic was the yellow-green color of the floor. . . . When I lived there I had hated that color, but now that I was to leave it I loved it with all my heart.

I noticed that the shelves and the wheeled kitchen cart were bare. But, in fact, everything had been packed away ages ago. Then I realized that Yuichi was there, cleaning the floor with a rag. I relaxed.

"Take a break, let's have some tea," I said. My voice echoed loudly in the empty apartment. It felt large, very large.

"Sure." Yuichi looked up. I thought, to work himself into such a sweat scrubbing the floor in a house someone else is moving out of . . . that's so like him.

"So this was your kitchen," Yuichi said, sitting on a cushion on the floor and drinking the tea I brought him from a glass (the teacups were all gone). "It must have been great."

"It was," I said. I was drinking, tea-ceremony style, with both hands, from a bowl.

It was as quiet as the inside of a glass case. Looking up, I saw that all that remained of the clock on the wall was its outline.

"What time is it?" I asked.

"Around midnight, I think," said Yuichi.

"How do you know?"

"It's so dark outside, and so quiet."

"I guess you could say I'm fleeing by night."

"To continue what we were talking about," said Yuichi. "Are you planning to move out from our place, too? Don't."

I looked at him, puzzled. It wasn't a continuation of anything we had been talking about.

"You seem to think that I live on impulse, like Eriko, but inviting you was something I thought over very carefully. Your grandmother was always so concerned about you, and probably the person who can best understand how you feel in this world is me. I know that once you're well again, really okay again, you'll do what you want. But for now leaving would be wrong. You don't have anyone but me who can tell you that. The money my mother has saved up from working so hard—that's what it's *for*, times like this. It's not only for buying juicers!" He laughed. "Please stay with us. Relax!"

He looked me straight in the eye and he spoke for all the world with the sincerity of someone trying to persuade a murderer to turn himself in.

I nodded.

"Well! I'm going to finish mopping the floor," he said.

As I washed the tea things, I heard Yuichi singing to himself, his voice blending in with the sound of running water.

> *To avoid disturbing the*
> *Moonlight shadows*

> *I brought my boat to rest*
> *At the tip of the cape*

"Oh!!" I said. "I know that song. What's it called again? I love that song. Who was it that sang it?"

"Umm . . . Momoko Sakuchi. It really sticks with you, doesn't it?" Yuichi smiled.

"Yes, yes!"

While I scrubbed the sink and Yuichi mopped, we sang together. It was so much fun, hearing our voices in the silent kitchen in the middle of the night.

"I especially love this part," I said, singing the second stanza.

> *A lighthouse in the distance*
> *To the two of us in the night*
> *The spinning light looks like*
> *Sunshine through the branches of trees*

In high spirits, we sang that part again, together, at the top of our lungs: "A LIGHTHOUSE IN THE DIS-TANCE—TO THE TWO OF US IN THE NIGHT THE SPINNING LIGHT LOOKS LIKE SUNSHINE THROUGH THE BRANCHES OF TREES."

All of a sudden I found myself blurting out: "Wait, *stop*. We're going to wake my grandmother sleeping in the next room." Now I've done it, I thought.

Yuichi seemed to feel it, too. He abruptly stopped scrubbing and turned to face me, his eyes troubled. Embarrassed, I tried to smile.

The son that Eriko had brought up so gently was suddenly revealed to be a prince. "After we finish cleaning up here, I really feel like stopping at the *ramen* noodle stand in the park," he said.

I awoke abruptly.

It's true that I wasn't used to going to bed so early, but that wasn't the reason. I went into the kitchen for a drink of water, thinking, strange dream. . . . My heart was chilled. Eriko wasn't home yet. It was two A.M.

The sensation of the dream was still very fresh. Listening to the sound of water splashing on the stainless steel, I wondered vacantly, should I scrub the sink? . . .

The night was so deathly silent that I felt I could hear the sound of the stars moving across the heavens. The glass of water soaked into my withered heart. It was chilly. My bare feet trembled in my slippers.

"Hi there." Coming up behind me, Yuichi made me jump.

"Wha–what?" I said, turning around.

"I just woke up and I'm starving. I was thinking, hmm, maybe I'll make some *ramen* noodles. . . ." In contrast to the way he had been in my dream, Yuichi was mumbling, his face puffy with sleep.

I could feel my own face swollen from crying. "I'll make it for you," I said. "Have a seat on my sofa."

"Ah," he said, "*your* sofa." He stumbled over to it and sat down.

In this little room suspended in the black of night, under the kitchen light, I opened the refrigerator. I chopped vegetables. Here in my favorite place, I suddenly thought: *ramen*! What a coincidence! Without turning around I said playfully, "In my dream you said you wanted *ramen*."

There was no response whatsoever. Wondering if he had fallen back asleep, I looked over, and there was Yuichi, gaping at me.

"I . . . I don't believe this," I said.

"The floor in your old kitchen, was it a kind of yellow-green color?" Yuichi asked. "This isn't some kind of riddle."

That was strange. I nodded and said, "Thanks for mopping it for me." Women are always quicker to pick up on these things.

"Now I'm awake," he said, but, half-apologetic for not getting it sooner, he smiled. "I really want you to make me some tea right now, and not in a teacup."

"You make it."

"Hmm," he said. "Okay, how about some juice—you want some?"

"Sure."

Yuichi went to the refrigerator and got out a couple of grapefruits, then happily took the juicer from its box. Accompanied by the ungodly racket of the machine in the silent, middle-of-the-night kitchen, I slipped the noodles into boiling water.

While what had happened was utterly amazing, it didn't seem so out of the ordinary, really. It was at once a miracle and the most natural thing in the world.

I held the feeling in my heart; the urge to discuss it died out. There was all the time in the world. In the endless repetition of other nights, other mornings, this moment, too, might become a dream.

"It's not easy being a woman," said Eriko one evening out of the blue.

I lifted my nose from the magazine I was reading and said, "Huh?" The beautiful Eriko was watering the plants in front of the terrace before she left for work.

"Because I have a lot of faith in you, I suddenly feel I ought to tell you something. I learned it raising Yuichi. There were many, many difficult times, god knows. If a person wants to stand on her own two feet, I recommend undertaking the care and feeding of something. It could be children, or it could be house plants, you know? By doing that you come to understand your own limitations. That's where it starts." As if chanting a liturgy, she related to me her philosophy of life.

"Life can be so hard," I said, moved.

"Yes. But if a person hasn't ever experienced true despair, she grows old never knowing how to evaluate where she is in life; never understanding what joy really is. I'm grateful for it."

Her hair rustled, brushing her shoulders. There are many days when all the awful things that happen make you sick at heart, when the path before you is so steep you can't bear to look. Not even love can rescue a person from that. Still, enveloped in the twilight coming from the west, there she was, watering the plants with her slender, graceful hands, in the midst of a light so sweet it seemed to form a rainbow in the transparent water she poured.

"I think I understand."

"I love your honest heart, Mikage. The grandmother who raised you must have been a wonderful person."

I smiled. "She was."

"You've been lucky," said Eriko. She laughed, her back to me.

One day I'll have to move out, I thought as I turned back to my magazine. The thought made me woozy. But I would have to do it.

Someday, I wondered, will I be living somewhere else and look back nostalgically on my time here? Or will I return to this same kitchen someday?

But right now I am here with this powerful mother, this boy with the gentle eyes. That was all that mattered.

As I grow older, much older, I will experience many things, and I will hit rock bottom again and again. Again and again I will suffer; again and again I will get back on my feet. I will not be defeated. I won't let my spirit be destroyed.

*   *   *

Dream kitchens.

I will have countless ones, in my heart or in reality. Or in my travels. Alone, with a crowd of people, with one other person—in all the many places I will live. I know that there will be so many more.

2 FULL MOON

Eriko died late in the autumn.

A crazy man became obsessed with her and killed her. He had spotted her on the street and liked what he saw; when he followed her he discovered that the place where she worked was a gay bar. Shocked to find out that this beautiful woman was a man, he began writing her long letters and hanging around the bar. The more persistent he was, the colder Eriko and the people at the club became. One night, screaming that he had been made a fool of, he lunged at her with a knife. Eriko, wounded, grabbed a barbell off the bar—it was part of the club's decor—with both hands and beat him to death.

"There!" she said. "Self-defense, that makes us even." Those were her last words.

I didn't learn of this until winter. It was a while before Yuichi finally phoned to let me know.

"She died fighting," Yuichi said without preamble. It was one o'clock in the morning. I jumped out of bed in the dark at the ring of the telephone and grabbed the receiver. I had no idea what he was talking about. In my sleepy brain I pictured a scene from a war movie.

"Yuichi? What? What are you talking about?"

After a long silence he said, "My mother . . . or, uh, father, I should say, was killed."

I didn't understand; nothing was getting through. I was too stunned to speak. As if reluctant to talk about it, he began to tell me about Eriko's death, little by little.

He spoke haltingly, but with each word the tale became more incredible. I stared into space. For a moment the receiver seemed miles away.

"When . . . did it happen? Recently?" I asked, though I had no idea where my own voice was coming from or what I was saying.

"No. It was a while back. Her friends at the club gave her a small funeral. I'm sorry. Somehow . . . somehow I just couldn't bring myself to call you."

I felt like my insides had been gouged out. And now she is no longer here. She isn't anywhere anymore.

"Forgive me, please forgive me," Yuichi kept repeating.

The telephone wasn't enough. I couldn't see him. Did he want to cry, did he want to laugh hysterically, did he want to have a long talk, did he want to be left alone? I couldn't tell.

"Yuichi, I'm coming over right now. Is that okay? I want to talk to you and I want to see your face when I talk to you."

"Sure. I'll drive you home so you won't have to worry about getting back in the middle of the night." Of course he had agreed without giving me a clue as to his emotional state.

"See you soon," I said, and hung up.

When was it that Eriko and I last saw each other? Had we parted laughing? My head was spinning. It was early in the fall when I left the university once and for all and got a job as an assistant in a cooking school. Was that the last time I had seen her, the day I moved out? Eriko had cried a little: "You're still going to be in the neighborhood— you'll come back and see us on weekends, won't you?" No, no, that wasn't it. I saw her near the end of last month. Yes, at the all-night minimart.

It was the middle of the night, and I couldn't sleep. I had gone to the store to get a pudding cup, and there was Eriko, just off work, standing in the doorway with the "girls" from the club, drinking coffee out of paper cups and eating fish balls in broth. I called out, "Eriko-san!"

She took my hand and said, "My goodness, Mikage, you've gotten so thin since you left our house!" She laughed. She was wearing a blue dress.

On my way out with the pudding, I saw her, cup in

hand, her eyes half-closed, watching the city glitter in the darkness. I said, teasing, "Eriko, you're looking a little masculine tonight!" She flashed me a big smile and said, "Poor me! I have a smart-ass for a daughter. I wonder if she's hitting puberty?" I answered that I was beyond that, thank you, and all the girls laughed. She asked me to come and visit soon, and I said I would. We parted smiling. That was the last time.

How long did it take me to put together an overnight bag? I was running around like a chicken with its head cut off. Opening and closing drawers, checking in the bathroom, breaking a vase, mopping it up. I covered the entire apartment several times over in total confusion. I smiled a little at how typical it was that I should still be empty-handed after all that frenzied activity. You have to calm down, I thought, and closed my eyes.

At last I stuffed a toothbrush and towel into the bag and, after double-checking that the gas was off and the answering machine on, I stumbled out of the apartment.

When I regained enough composure to realize where I was, I found I was walking up the wintry street toward the Tanabes' apartment building. As I walked along under the starry sky, my keys jingling, the tears began to flow one after the other. The street, my footsteps, the quiet buildings, everything seemed warped. My breath became painfully blocked; I felt like I was choking. My eyes were stung by the lashing wind, and I began to feel colder and colder.

Things that my eyes normally take in—telephone poles,

street lights, parked cars, the black sky—I could now barely make out. There was a strange beauty to their distortion. Everything came zooming in at me. I felt powerless to stop the energy from rushing out of my body; it seemed to dissipate with a hissing sound into the darkness.

When my parents died I was still a child. When my grandfather died, I had a boyfriend. When my grandmother died I was left all alone. But never had I felt so alone as I did now.

From the bottom of my heart, I wanted to give up; I wanted to give up on living. There was no denying that tomorrow would come, and the day after tomorrow, and so next week, too. I never thought it would be this hard, but I would go on living in the midst of a gloomy depression, and that made me feel sick to the depths of my soul. In spite of the tempest raging within me, I walked the night path calmly.

I wanted it to end, and quickly, but for now I would go see Yuichi. Hear everything he had to say, in detail. But what good would that do? What could come of it? It was not a question of hoping for anything. It would mean being flooded with an even more gigantic despair. Utterly devoid of hope, I rang the doorbell. In my confusion I had run up the stairs all the way to the tenth floor before I even realized it, and I was panting.

I listened to the familiar rhythm of his footsteps approaching the door. When I was living there I had often gone out and forgotten my key—I don't know how many times I had rung that doorbell in the middle of the night. Yuichi would get out of bed and come to the door, and the sound of the chain would echo in the silent hallway the way it did now.

"Hi." A somewhat thinner Yuichi greeted me.

"It's been a long time," I said, unable to repress a big smile. In spite of myself I was glad. In the inner recesses of my heart I was unabashedly happy to see him.

He just stood there, gaping. "May I come in?" I asked. He smiled weakly and said, as if recovering himself, "Sure, of course. I was . . . I um . . . I was expecting you to be incredibly mad at me. Sorry. Please come in."

"How could I be mad? You should know me better than that."

Yuichi said, "Right," trying to show me his old grin. I smiled back at him and took off my shoes in the entryway.

At first I was strangely ill at ease in this apartment where I had lived until just a little while ago, and I was seized with nostalgia. But I sank into the sofa and soon became reacclimated to its smells. Yuichi brought me coffee.

"It feels like ages since I've been here."

"It does, doesn't it? You must have been pretty busy. How's your job? Is it fun?" asked Yuichi politely.

"Yes, right now everything I do is fun, you know? Even peeling potatoes. I'm still in that phase," I answered, smiling. Then, putting down his cup, Yuichi started to talk.

"Tonight, for the first time, my brain started working again, and I realized that I had to tell you. So I called."

I leaned forward attentively, looking into his eyes.

"Up to the funeral, I couldn't take in what had happened. My mind was blank; in my eyes everything was dark. I'd never lived with anyone but Eriko. She was my mother, my father. Because she was always just Eriko, I never had to think about it; there were so many things to do every day that I just kept barrelling along without worrying about it. That's how things were. And then, wow! At the funeral . . . It was so like her, not to die in some normal way. Even the murderer's wife and kids showed up. The girls from the club went nuts, and had I not behaved in a way befitting an eldest son it would have been complete chaos. You've been on my mind the whole time. That's the truth. All the time. But somehow I just couldn't call you. I was afraid that telling you would make it all real. I mean, to have my mother, my father, die that way meant I was left all alone. I couldn't tell you, even though I knew that you two were close. I was confused, out of my mind." Yuichi was staring at the cup in his hand.

I looked intently at his face, so beaten down by it all, and this is what came out of my mouth: "For some reason there's always death around us. My parents, my grandfather, my grandmother . . . your real mother, even Eriko. My god—in this gigantic universe there can't be a pair like us. The fact that we're friends is amazing. All this death . . . all this death."

"Really." Yuichi smiled. "Maybe we should go into business. Our clients could pay us to move in with people they want dead. We'll call ourselves *de*struction workers."

His sadly cheerful face radiated a dim glow. We moved deeper into the dead of night. I turned around to look out the window at the flickering lights below. The city was fringed with tiny points of brightness, and the lines of cars were like a phosphorescent river flowing through the darkness.

"So I've become an orphan," said Yuichi.

"That goes double for me. Not that I'm bragging about it," I said, laughing, and suddenly tears began to stream down Yuichi's cheeks.

"I really needed you to make me laugh," he said, rubbing his eyes with his arm, "so much I couldn't stand it anymore."

I reached out and took his face in both hands. "Thank you for calling me," I said softly.

We decided that I should have Eriko's favorite red sweater. I recalled the evening when I had tried it on, and she had said, "God, how it pains me! Expensive as it was, it looks much better on you."

Then Yuichi went to Eriko's dresser drawer and pulled out her amazingly lengthy "will." After handing it to me, he bid me goodnight and went to his room. I read:

Yuichi,

I feel very odd writing a letter to my own child. But because lately I've been feeling that somehow I might be in danger, I'm writing you this on the one chance in a million that something might happen to me. No, just kidding. One of these days we'll read this together and laugh.

Yuichi, think about what I'm about to say. If I

should die, you will be left all alone. But you have Mikage, don't you? I'm not joking about that girl. We have no relatives. When I married your mother, her parents cut off relations entirely. And then, when I became a woman, they cursed me. So I'm asking you, DON'T, whatever you do, DO NOT contact them, ever. Do you understand me?

Yes, Yuichi, in this world there are all kinds of people. There are people who choose to live their lives in filth; this is hard for me to understand. People who purposely do abhorrent things, just for the attention it draws to them, until they themselves are trapped. I cannot understand it, and no matter how much they suffer I cannot feel pity for them. But I have cheerfully chosen to make my body my fortune. I am *beautiful*! I am *dazzling*! If people I don't care for are attracted to me, I accept it as the wages of beauty. So, if I should be killed, it will be an accident. Don't get any strange ideas. Believe in the me that you knew.

Just this once I wanted to write using men's language, and I've really tried. But it's funny—I get embarrassed and the pen won't go. I guess I thought that even though I've lived all these years as a woman, somewhere inside me was my male self, that I've been playing a role all these years. But I find that I'm body and soul a woman. A mother in name and in fact. I have to laugh.

I have loved my life. My years as a man, my years married to your mother, and after she died, becoming and living as a woman, watching you grow up, living together so happily, and—oh! taking Mikage in!! That was the most fun of all, wasn't it? I yearn to see her again. She, too, is a very precious child of mine.

Sentimental of me, isn't it?

Please tell her I said hi. And tell her to stop bleaching the hair on her legs in front of boys. It's indecent. Don't you think so?

You'll find enclosed the papers detailing all my assets. I know you can't make heads or tails of all that legalese. Call the lawyer, okay? In any case, I've left everything to you except the club. Isn't it great being an only child?

XXX

Eriko

When I finished reading I carefully refolded the letter. The smell of Eriko's favorite perfume tugged at my heart. This, too, will disappear after the letter is opened a few more times, I thought. That was hardest of all.

I stretched out on the sofa that had been my bed when I lived here, feeling a nostalgia so sharp it was painful. Night was just as it had been—here I was in the same room, the silhouettes of the plants in front of the terrace window looking down over the city.

Still, no matter how late I waited up, she would not come back.

Just before dawn: the sound of humming and high-heeled shoes drawing nearer, the key in the door. After the club closed she would come home a little tipsy, and because she made a lot of noise, I would wake up, sleepy-eyed. When I heard the sound of the shower, the sound of her slippers, the sound of water boiling, I would go back to sleep, feeling at peace. It was always like that. How I missed her! So much I thought I'd go mad.

I wondered if I'd woken Yuichi with my crying—or was he in the throes of a heavy, painful dream?

A door opened before us that night—the door to the grave.

The next day both of us slept into the afternoon. I had the day off and was nibbling bread and lazily looking through the newspaper when Yuichi came out of his room. After washing his face, he sat down beside me and poured himself a glass of milk. "I guess I'll go to class now. . . ."

"My, you students have a cushy life, don't you?" I broke my bread in half for him. "Thanks," he said, taking it and eating it noisily. I had the strange sensation, while we were sitting in front of the TV, that we really were orphans.

"Mikage," he said, getting up, "are you going back to your house tonight?"

"Hmm . . ." I thought about it. "I wonder if I should go home after dinner. . . ."

"Ah!" said Yuichi, "make me a professional dinner!" That gave me a terrific idea, and I got serious.

"All right, then, let's get to work. We'll make a dinner to end all dinners."

I enthusiastically planned a magnificent feast, wrote

down everything we needed, and thrust the paper at him.

"Take the car. Buy everything on this list and bring it back. I'm going to make all your favorite foods, so I hope you'll be quick about it, since the sooner you get back, the sooner you'll be digging in."

"Ordering me around like a new bride," he grumbled on his way out.

I heard the door close, and when I was alone I realized I was dead tired. The room was so unearthly quiet, I lost all sense of time being divided into seconds. I felt that I was the only person alive and moving in a world brought to a stop.

Houses always feel like that after someone has died.

I sank into the sofa and stared blankly at the melancholy early-winter gray outside the large window. The heavy, cold air of winter permeated every part of this little neigh-borhood—the park, the walkways—like a fog. I couldn't bear it. It oppressed me, and I felt like I couldn't breathe.

Truly great people emit a light that warms the hearts of those around them. When that light has been put out, a heavy shadow of despair descends. Perhaps Eriko's was only a minor kind of greatness, but her light was sorely missed.

I flopped down on my back and looked up at the dear, familiar ceiling. Right after my grandmother died, I had stared at this same ceiling many an afternoon while Yuichi and Eriko were out. I remember thinking to myself, my grandmother is dead, I've lost my last blood relation, and things can't get any worse. But now they had. Eriko had been enormously important to me. In the six months we spent together she had always been there for me; she spoiled me.

To the extent that I had come to understand that despair does not necessarily result in annihilation, that one can go on as usual in spite of it, I had become hardened. Was that what it means to be an adult, to live with ugly ambiguities? I didn't like it, but it made it easier to go on.

My heart was so heavy now because of just that. I watched the gloomy clouds and the orange of the sunset spreading across them in the western sky. Soon the cold night would descend and fill the hollow in my heart. I felt sleepy but said to myself, if you sleep now, you'll have bad dreams. So I got up.

After a long absence I was once again in the Tanabe kitchen. For an instant I had a vision of Eriko's smiling face, and my heart turned over. I felt an urge to get moving. It looked to me like the kitchen had not been used in quite a while. It was somewhat dirty and dark. I began to clean. I scrubbed the sink with scouring powder, wiped off the burners, washed the dishes, sharpened the knives. I washed and bleached all the dish towels, and while watching them go round and round in the dryer I realized that I had become calmer. Why do I love everything that has to do with kitchens so much? It's strange. Perhaps because to me a kitchen represents some distant longing engraved on my soul. As I stood there, I seemed to be making a new start; something was coming back.

★   ★   ★

That summer I had taught myself to cook.

The sensation that my brain cells were multiplying was exhilarating. I bought three books on cooking—fundamentals, theory, and practice—and went through them one by one. On the bus, in bed, on the sofa, I read the one on theory, memorizing caloric content, temperatures, and raw ingredients. Every spare minute I cooked. Those three books grew tattered with use, and even now I always have them near at hand. Like the picture books I loved when I was little, I know the illustrations on each page by heart.

Yuichi and Eriko took to saying to each other, "Mikage has gone completely nuts, hasn't she?" And it's true that for the whole summer I went about it with a crazed enthusiasm: cooking, cooking, cooking. I poured all my earnings from my part-time job into it, and if something came out wrong I'd do it over till I got it right. Angry, fretful, or cheery, I cooked through it all.

When I think about it now, it was because of my cooking that the three of us ate together as often as we did; it was a good summer.

Looking out the window as the evening wind came through the screen door, a remnant of pale blue stretching over the hot sky, we ate boiled pork, cold Chinese noodles, cucumber salad. I cooked for them: she who made a fuss over everything I did; he who ate vast quantities in silence.

Complicated omelets, beautifully shaped vegetables

cooked in broth, tempura—it took a fair amount of work to be able to make those things. Because my biggest flaw is lack of precision, it didn't occur to me that dishes turn out badly or well in proportion to one's attention to detail. For example, if I put something in the oven before it had come to temperature, or if I got the steam going before I had everything chopped, that sort of triviality (or so I thought) was precisely reflected in the color and shape of the final product. Which surprised me. Although that kind of cooking made my dinners no worse than those of the average housewife, they by no means resembled the illustrations in the books.

There was only one way to learn: I tried making anything and everything, and I tried to do it right. I would carefully wipe out the bowls, replace the caps on the spices every time, calmly chart out the steps in advance, and when I began to make myself crazy with irritation I would stop what I was doing and take a few deep breaths. At first my impatience would lead me to the brink of despair, but when I finally learned to correct my mistakes coolly, it was truly as if I had somehow reformed my own slapdash character. Or so I felt (of course, it wasn't true).

Getting the job I have now, as an assistant to a cooking teacher, was incredible. She not only teaches cooking classes, but also gets a lot of important television and magazine work, and she is actually rather famous. An amazing number of candidates apparently tested for the job. Why was it that I—a novice with only one summer of study under my belt—got hired? When I saw the women who attend the classes, it made sense. Their attitude was completely different from mine.

Those women lived their lives happily. They had been taught, probably by caring parents, not to exceed the boundaries of their happiness regardless of what they were doing. But therefore they could never know real joy. Which is better? Who can say? Everyone lives the way she knows best. What I mean by "their happiness" is living a life untouched as much as possible by the knowledge that we are really, all of us, alone. That's not a bad thing. Dressed in their aprons, their smiling faces like flowers, learning to cook, absorbed in their little troubles and perplexities, they fall in love and marry. I think that's great. I wouldn't mind that kind of life. Me, when I'm utterly exhausted by it all, when my skin breaks out, on those lonely evenings when I call my friends again and again and nobody's home, then I despise my own life—my birth, my upbringing, everything. I feel only regret for the whole thing.

But—that one summer of bliss. In that kitchen.

I was not afraid of burns or scars; I didn't suffer from sleepless nights. Every day I thrilled with pleasure at the challenges tomorrow would bring. Memorizing the recipe, I would make carrot cakes that included a bit of my soul. At the supermarket I would stare at a bright red tomato, loving it for dear life. Having known such joy, there was no going back.

No matter what, I want to continue living with the awareness that I will die. Without that, I am not alive. That is what makes the life I have now possible.

Inching one's way along a steep cliff in the dark: on reaching the highway, one breathes a sigh of relief. Just when one can't take any more, one sees the moonlight. Beauty that seems to infuse itself into the heart: I know about that.

It was evening by the time I'd finished cleaning up and preparing for dinner.

Yuichi rang the doorbell and, carrying a large plastic bag in his arms, pushed the door open with a great show of difficulty and stuck his head inside. I walked toward him.

"Unbelievable," he said, putting down his burden with a thud.

"What is?"

"I bought everything you said to, but I can't carry it all in one trip. There's too much."

"Oh," I said, pretending not to catch on, but Yuichi's snort of irritation let me know there was no getting out of it. I went down with him to the garage.

In the car were two more gigantic bags. Even carrying them from the car to the garage entrance was backbreaking.

"I bought a few things for myself, too," said Yuichi, carrying the heavier of the two.

"A few things?" I peered into my bag. Besides shampoo and notebooks, there were lots of "instant" dinners: a clear indication of his recent eating habits.

"You could have made a couple of trips."

"Yes, but—with you we can do it in one. Hey, look! Isn't that a pretty moon?" Yuichi pointed to the winter moon with his chin.

"Oh, isn't it," I said sarcastically (his diversionary tactics were so obvious), but as I stepped into the building I turned to glance at it. It was almost full and shed an incredible brightness.

In the elevator on the way up, Yuichi said, "Of course there's a relationship."

"Between what?"

"Don't you think that seeing such a beautiful moon influences what one cooks? But not in the sense of 'moon-viewing *udon*,' for instance."

The elevator stopped with a little jerk. When he said that, my heart faltered for an instant. He spoke as if he knew my very soul. As we walked to the door, I asked, "In what sense then? In a more profound way?"

"Yes, yes. In a more human sense, you know?"

"I agree. That's absolutely true," I said without hesitation. If they asked a hundred people on a quiz show, a hundred voices would reverberate as one: "Yes! Yes! It's true!"

"You know that I think of you as an artist. For you cooking is an art. You really do love to work in the kitchen. Of course you do. Good thing, too."

Yuichi agreed with himself again and again, carrying on a one-man conversation. I said, smiling, "You're just like a child."

A moment before, my heart had seemed to stop. Now that feeling voiced itself in my mind: If Yuichi is with me,

I need nothing else. It flashed for only an instant, but it left me extremely confused, dazzled as I was by the light given off by his eyes.

It took me two hours to make dinner.

Yuichi peeled potatoes and watched TV while I cooked. He had very nimble fingers.

For me, Eriko's death was still a distant event. I couldn't deal with it head-on. Faced with a tempest of shock, I could only approach the dark fact of her death little by little. And Yuichi—Yuichi was like a willow beaten down by the driving rain.

So even though it was now just the two of us, we avoided talking about Eriko's death, and that omission loomed larger and larger in time and space. But for the time being, "just the two of us" was a warm, safe place where the future was on hold. And yet there was—how should I put this?—a huge, terrifying premonition that those unpaid bills would inexorably come due. The enormity of it only heightened our feeling of being orphans alone in the dark.

The limpid night descended, and we began to eat the extravagant dinner I had prepared. Salad, pie, stew, croquettes. Deep-fried tofu, steamed greens, bean thread with chicken (each with their various sauces), Chicken Kiev, sweet-and-sour pork, steamed Chinese dumplings . . . It was an international hodge-podge, but we ate it all (it took hours), with wine, until we couldn't face another bite.

Yuichi, uncharacteristically, was very drunk. Just as I

was thinking that it was odd—I didn't see him have that much at dinner—I noticed, with a start, an empty bottle on the floor. Apparently he had been at it while I was cooking; no wonder he was three sheets to the wind. I asked him, amazed, "Yuichi, did you drink this whole bottle before dinner?"

Yuichi, face up on the sofa, munching celery, muttered, "Yup."

"You hid it well," I said, and Yuichi's face suddenly looked terribly sad. It's tough dealing with things when you're drunk. "What's wrong?" I asked.

Yuichi said, his face serious, "That's all everyone has been saying for the last month, and it really hurts."

"Everyone? You mean at school?"

"Yeah, more or less."

"Have you been drinking like this for a month?"

"Yeah."

"No wonder you didn't feel like calling me," I said, laughing.

"The telephone was *glowing*." He laughed, too. "I'd be walking home at night, drunk, and I'd see a phone booth, all lit up. Even on a dark street I could always see a telephone booth in the distance. I would sort of tortuously make my way over to it, thinking, I have to call Mikage, and I'd repeat your number in my head, get out my telephone card, step into the booth, and everything. But then, just on the verge of dialing, when I'd think about the state I was in, and what I would say, I'd stop. Then I'd go home and collapse into bed and have these horrible dreams where I'd call you and you'd be crying and angry with me."

"It was all your imagination. And imagination is sometimes worse than reality."

"You're right. Suddenly I feel happy." In a sleepy voice, he continued, pausing frequently. He probably had no idea what he was saying. "You came to this apartment even though my mother is dead. I thought you'd be angry with me and never want to see me again. It was something I was prepared for, if that was how it had to be. I was afraid that the memory of the three of us living here might just be too painful. I had a feeling I would never see you again." Yuichi breathed a sigh of relief and continued, as though he were talking to himself. "I always liked it when people stayed here on the sofa. The crisp white sheets and all . . . Even though we were at home, it was like being on a trip. . . . Since I've been alone in this place, I haven't been eating very well. I'd often say to myself, hmm, should I cook something? But food, too, was giving off light, like the telephone. So I wondered if eating would put out the light, but it seemed like too much trouble, so I just drank. I thought maybe if I explain everything to Mikage, she'll come over, maybe not move back in, but just come over. At least maybe she'll listen to what I have to say. But I was afraid—terribly afraid—to even hope for such happiness. If I did let myself hope for that, and you became angry with me, I'd be pushed even further toward the depth of despair. I didn't have the confidence, the courage, to explain all this to you so you could understand what was going on with me."

"That's so like you." My tone was angry, but my eyes betrayed tenderness. In the time we had spent together, we had come to share a deep understanding, a kind of telepathy. Despite the alcohol, I had conveyed the complexity of my feelings.

"I wish today could never end," he continued. "I wish this night would go on forever. Mikage, please move back in."

"That's a possibility," I said, making an effort to be gentle. I was sure he was just talking drunken foolishness. "But Eriko isn't here anymore. If I were to live here with you, would it be as your lover? Or your friend?"

"You mean, should we sell the sofa and buy a double bed?" Yuichi smiled. Then he said, frankly, "I myself don't even know." Oddly, his sincerity touched me most of all. He continued, "Right now I can't think. What do you mean in my life? How am I myself changing? How will my life be different from before? I don't have a clue about any of that. I try to think about it, but with the kind of worthless thoughts I'm having in the state I'm in, I can't decide anything. I've got to pull myself out of it soon. Now I've got *you* tangled up in it. The two of us may be in the epicenter of death, but I was hoping to spare you this misery. It could be like this for as long as we stay together."

"Yuichi, don't think like that. Let's see what happens," I said, on the verge of tears.

"Right. I won't remember any of this tomorrow. It's always like that. No day has any connection to the one before."

With that he flopped down on his stomach, muttering, "I'm in a bad way. . . ."

The apartment had taken on the silence of the dead of

night and seemed as though it were listening to Yuichi's voice. It was lost without Eriko. The feeling bore down heavier as the night deepened. It made me feel that nothing could be shared.

Yuichi and I are climbing a narrow ladder in the jet-black gloom. Together we peer into the cauldron of hell. We stare into the bubbling red sea of fire, and the air hitting our faces is so hot it makes us reel. Even though we're standing side by side, even though we're closer to each other than to anyone else in the world, even though we're friends forever, we don't join hands. No matter how forlorn we are, we each insist on standing on our own two feet. But I wonder, as I look at his uneasy profile blazingly illuminated by the hellish fire, although we have always acted like brother and sister, aren't we really man and woman in the primordial sense, and don't we think of each other that way? But the place we are in now is just too dreadful. It is not a place where two people can create a life together.

Although I had been earnestly daydreaming until then, I suddenly started to laugh. "I see two lovers looking over the edge of the cauldron of hell. Are they contemplating a double suicide? This means their love will end in hell." I couldn't stop laughing.

I was certainly no fortune-teller.

Yuichi was fast asleep on the sofa. From the smile on his face he seemed pleased to have fallen asleep before me. He didn't bat an eyelash when I pulled a quilt over him.

I washed the enormous pile of dirty dishes as quietly as

possible, and I cried and cried. Of course it wasn't over having to wash all those dishes; I was crying for having been left behind in the night, paralyzed with loneliness.

I awoke the next morning to the god-awful ring of the alarm clock I had staunchly set the night before, since I had to be at work at noon. When I stretched my hand out to turn it off, I realized it was the telephone. I answered, "Hello," and then, immediately recalling I was at somebody else's house, I added, flustered, "Tanabe residence."

The party on the other end hung up with a crash. Aha, I thought—a girl. I sheepishly looked over at Yuichi, but he was still sound asleep. So much the better, I thought. I got dressed, slipped out of the apartment, and headed for work. I had the whole afternoon to agonize over whether or not to stay there that night.

I made my way to my job. The operation occupied an entire floor in a large building, what with *Sensei*'s office, the kitchens, and the photo studio. *Sensei* was in her office checking over the proofs of a magazine article. Still a young woman, she had a great sense of style and a wonderful way with people. When she saw me she smiled, removed her glasses, and began to give me the rundown on the day's tasks.

Because today there was a huge amount of prep work for the classes that would begin at three o'clock, she asked me to help and told me that I could go home after we were done. Apparently the head assistant would take over for the evening classes, so I would be finished early. I was almost disappointed, when she then made a proposal that was perfectly timed for my current dilemma.

"Mikage," she said, "the day after tomorrow we have to go to the Izu Peninsula to do some research. We'll be staying three nights. I know this is short notice, but if at all possible I wonder if you'd mind coming along."

"Izu?" I asked, surprised. "Is this for a magazine?"

"Well . . . the thing is, the other girls have scheduling conflicts. We're planning on going to sample the specialties of a number of inns, and they'll also tell us something about their preparation. How does that strike you? We'll be staying in very nice places—traditional inns and hotels. You'd have a room to yourself. But I need an answer as soon as possible—say, by tonight?"

Before she'd even finished, I said, "I'll go!" With that I answered both her question and the one I had planned to ponder.

"I really appreciate it," said *Sensei* with a smile.

As I walked toward the cooking class, I suddenly realized that a weight had been lifted from me. Right now, getting away from Tokyo, away from Yuichi, to put some distance between us for a little while, struck me as a very good thing.

When I opened the door, I saw that Nori and Kuri, two of my fellow assistants, my seniors on the job by a year, were already at work on the preparations.

"Mikage," said Kuri as soon as she saw me, "did you hear about Izu?"

Nori smiled. "Sounds great, doesn't it? There's going to

be French food and all kinds of seafood, too."

"Yes. But by the way, why is it *I* get to go?"

"Oh—I'm sorry. We're both scheduled for golf lessons, so we can't. But really, if you can't do it, one of us will just miss a lesson. Right, Kuri? It's okay."

"Yes, that's right, Mikage, so be honest with us."

I smiled—both of them were so sincerely sweet—and shook my head. "No, no," I assured them, "it's really fine with me."

They had come to work here together after graduating from the same university. Naturally, having done four years of culinary study, they were real pros.

Kuri's sunny disposition lent her an appealing cuteness, and Nori was a beauty of the "proper young lady" variety. They were best friends. Their clothes were always in the best of taste, the kind that you can't help but stare at. They were even-tempered, considerate, and patient. Of their type—that is, young ladies of good family, hardly a rarity in the culinary world—they were the genuine article.

Once in a while Nori's mother would telephone. She was so gentle and kind she made me feel shy. What amazed me was that she usually seemed to know Nori's schedule for the entire day. But then I guess all mothers are like that.

Nori would talk to her on the phone in a voice like a silver bell, smiling a little smile and smoothing her long, fluttering hair.

As different as Kuri and Nori were from me, I liked them immensely. Just for handing them a ladle, they would smile and say thank you. If I had a cold they would immediately be all concern. The sight of them giggling, their white aprons brilliant in the light, made me happy. Working side by side with them was a pleasure that put me at peace with the world.

Dividing ingredients into bowls, bringing giant vats of water to a boil, measuring—doing routine work until three o'clock suited me fine. This sunny, large-windowed room, those big tables lined up in front of the ovens, the broilers and burners, reminded me of the home-ec rooms at school.

We gossiped, having fun as we worked.

It happened just a little after two. Unexpectedly, someone knocked very hard at the door.

"That might be *Sensei*." Nori looked up, puzzled. "Come in?" she said hesitantly.

Kuri whispered nervously, "I've forgotten to remove my nail polish! I'll get in trouble!" I bent down, looking for the nail polish remover in my bag.

The door opened, and we heard a girl's voice say, "Is there a Mikage Sakurai here?" I stood up quickly, surprised to hear my name. In the doorway was a girl I had never seen before.

Her face was a little babyish. I thought she was probably younger than me. She was small, and her eyes were round and hard. She stood her ground staunchly, wearing beige pumps and a brown coat over a thin yellow sweater. Her legs were sexy, if a little chubby. Her whole person had that roundness to it. Her narrow forehead was completely exposed, her bangs carefully curled back. Atop the supple curves of her body, her red-painted lips were angrily set.

I was worried. She didn't seem unlikable, but . . . I

couldn't imagine what she might have come for, although the reason was definitely not trivial.

Nori and Kuri, distressed, watched her from behind my back. I had to say something.

"Excuse me, but who are you?"

"My name is Okuno. I've come to speak with you." Her voice was hoarse but high-pitched.

"I'm sorry, but I'm working right now. Would you mind calling me tonight at home?"

"At Yuichi's house, you mean?" she piped up. At last I understood. She was this morning's hang-up caller. I said with conviction, "No, at my house."

Nori interjected: "Mikage, it's okay to go out. We'll tell *Sensei* you had to do some last-minute shopping for the trip."

"That won't be necessary. We'll be finished very soon," said the girl.

"Are you a friend of Yuichi Tanabe's?" I asked, making an effort to remain calm.

"Yes, I'm a classmate at the university. I came here today because I have something to ask of you. I'll be clear about it. Stay out of Yuichi's life."

"That's up to Yuichi," I said. "Even if you are his girlfriend, it doesn't strike me as something you should decide for him."

She turned red with anger. "Do you think what you're doing is right? You say you're not his girlfriend, yet you go over there whenever you want, you spend the night, you do what you please, don't you? That's *worse* than living together." Her eyes had filled with tears. "I never lived with him, I'm just a classmate; of course you know him better than I do. But in my own way, I love him. I comforted him when his mother died. A while back, when I told him how all this bothered me, he just said, 'So what about Mikage?' 'Is she your girlfriend?' I asked. 'Let's not talk about it now,' he said. Then, since the entire school knew there was a girl living at his house, I just dropped the whole thing."

I started to say, "I'm not living there anymore . . ." but she interrupted me. "You don't accept the responsibilities of a relationship. You just like to have fun and you keep him tied to you. Parading your slender arms and legs, your long hair, in front of him, never letting him forget your womanhood—thanks to you, Yuichi is half a man. That would really suit you, wouldn't it, to leave things undecided forever? But love is not a joke, it also means sharing someone else's pain. To slip that burden, with that cool face of yours, saying you understand everything. . . . I'm asking you, please, don't see Yuichi anymore. I'm begging you. Because as long as you're around, Yuichi is stuck."

Her insights were pretty self-serving, but because the violence of her words hit me exactly where it hurt, I was deeply pained. She was about to continue. I saw her open her mouth again, and I yelled, "Stop!"

She shut up, startled. I said, "I understand what you mean, but we each have to face our own feelings. What you say doesn't take into account any of mine. How can you be so sure, when you don't even know me, that I don't think about these things?"

"How can you speak so coldly?" She answered my

question with a question, tears streaming down her face.

"You say you've loved Yuichi all along?" I said. "With that attitude, I can't believe it. I just heard about his mother's death and I was sleeping over because of that. You're not being fair."

My heart filled with a terrible sadness. Surely she didn't want to hear about how Eriko had taken me into their home, about the emotional state I had been in at the time, about the complicated, fragile relationship I had with Yuichi now. She had only come to blame me. So even though I wasn't a rival, after this morning's phone call she must have asked around about me, found out where I worked, and ridden the train here, from somewhere far away, no doubt. All for a depressing mission that could offer her no solace. When I imagined the workings of her mind, the senseless anger that spurred her to come here, I pitied her from the bottom of my heart.

"I'm not insensitive," I said. "I know what it's like to lose someone. But this isn't the place to talk about it. If you have anything more to say . . ." I was about to tell her to call me at home, but instead I ended up blurting out, ". . . or perhaps you'd like me to sob hysterically and chase you with a kitchen knife?" I admit that it was rather cold-blooded of me. She gave me an evil scowl and said in a chilly voice, "I've said all I had to say. Excuse me." Those were her parting words. With the click, click of her little beige pumps, she turned and walked to the door. Then, slamming it with a bang, she was gone.

It was over, leaving behind the bitter aftertaste of a confrontation in which nothing was gained.

"Mikage, you did nothing wrong." Kuri came to my side, looking concerned.

"Yes," said Nori, peering kindly into my eyes. "She's insane. I think she's gone a little crazy with jealousy. Cheer up, Mikage."

In the afternoon sunlight of the kitchen, I found myself feeling immensely tired.

That evening I went back to the Tanabe apartment for my toothbrush and towel. Yuichi was out. I made myself some instant curry and ate it alone.

Cooking and eating in this house felt natural, almost too natural. I was absently mulling over my conversation with the girl when he came home. "Hi," he said.

Even though he couldn't know what had happened, and although I had done nothing wrong, I couldn't meet his eyes. "Yuichi, I just found out I have to go to Izu, for work, the day after tomorrow. I left my apartment in a mess the other night and I must go home and straighten up before the trip, so I think I'll stay there tonight. Oh— there's some curry left, help yourself."

"I see. Okay, I'll give you a ride," he said, smiling.

We set off in the car. The city flew past. We'd be at my place in another five minutes.

"Yuichi?"

"Hmm?"

"Umm . . . Let's . . . let's go have tea."

"I thought you were in such a hurry to pack and everything. It's fine with me, though."

"I have this incredible craving for tea."

"Let's do it. Where do you want to go?"

"You know that barley-tea shop above the beauty parlor?"

"Isn't that a little far? It's clear across town."

"I just have a feeling that's the best place."

"Okay, why not?" Even if it didn't make any sense to him, he was being very nice about it. Because he could see I wasn't feeling so hot, if I mentioned wanting to see the moon over Arabia right now, he'd say, "Let's go."

The little second-floor tea shop was quiet and cheerful. Surrounded by white walls, the place was warm and toasty. We sat down across from each other at the innermost table. There were no other customers. Movie sound-track music was playing faintly.

"Yuichi, when I think about it, isn't this the first time we've ever been to a café together? It's very strange."

"Is that right?" His eyes widened. He was drinking smelly Earl Grey whose soapy odor reminded me of many a late night at the Tanabes'. I'd be watching television with the sound down low in the dead quiet of midnight, and Yuichi would come out of his room to make tea.

In the uncertain ebb and flow of time and emotions, much of one's life history is etched in the senses. And things of no particular importance, or irreplaceable things, can suddenly resurface in a café one winter night.

"We've drunk so much tea together," said Yuichi. "At first I thought it couldn't be true that we haven't been to a café together, but come to think of it, it is."

"Funny, isn't it." I smiled.

"Nothing, nothing at all has any flavor for me now," said Yuichi, staring at the lamp on the table. "I must be really tired."

"That's only natural," I said, somewhat surprised.

"When your grandmother died you were like this, too. I remember it well. We'd be watching TV or whatever, and you'd say, like, 'What are they saying,' and I'd look up at you and you'd have this expression on your face, like your mind was blank. Now I understand completely."

"Yuichi," I said, "the fact that you're relaxed enough with me now to tell me how you're really feeling is a source of comfort to me. It makes me very happy. So happy I feel like shouting it from the rooftops."

"What kind of talk is that? Sounds like it was translated from English." Yuichi smiled, the light from the table lamp shining on his face. His shoulders shook beneath his navy blue sweater.

"It does, doesn't it? If . . ." I wanted to say, "If there's anything I can do, just say so," but I stopped myself. I silently implored: May the memory of this moment, here, the glowing impression of the two of us facing each other in this warm, bright place, drinking lovely hot tea, help save him, even a little bit.

Words, too explicit, always cast a shadow over that faint glow. Outside, night had come. The indigo-colored air was growing colder.

Whenever we got in the car, he would always open my door first and get me seated before he climbed in the driver's side.

I mentioned it as we pulled out. "There aren't many

men who will open a car door for a woman. I think it's really great."

"Eriko raised me that way," he said, laughing. "If I didn't open the door for her, she'd get mad and refuse to get in the car."

"Even though she was a man!" I said, laughing.

"Right, right, even though she was a man."

With that, silence fell with a thud.

It was night in the city. We watched the people come and go while we waited at the light: businessmen and office girls, young people and old, all beautifully aglow in the headlights. Enveloped in the silent cold, bundled in sweaters and coats—it was the hour when everyone was headed for someplace warm.

Then it suddenly occurred to me—Yuichi must have opened the car door for that awful girl as well. Inexplicably, my seatbelt seemed too tight. I realized with amazement—oh! This must be jealousy. Like children when they first learn why people say "ouch," this was my first experience of it. Now that Eriko was dead, the two of us, alone, were flowing down that river of light, suspended in the cosmic darkness, and were approaching a critical juncture.

I understood. I understood it from the color of the sky, the shape of the moon, the blackness of the night sky under which we passed. The building lights, the streetlights, were unforgiving.

He stopped in front of my house. "So," he said, "be sure to bring me back something." After this he'd be going back to that apartment, alone. Soon, no doubt, he'd be watering his plants.

77

"An eel pie, of course." I laughed.

His profile was dimly illuminated by the streetlights.

"An eel pie? You mean those coiled pastries? You can buy those at any food stand."

"Well, then . . . some tea, perhaps?"

"Hmm . . . how about some pickled *wasabi* root?"

"*Really*? I can't stand the stuff. Do you like it?"

"Only the kind with roe in it."

"Okay, that's what I'll bring you." I smiled and opened the car door.

Suddenly a freezing draft came blowing in.

"It's cold!" I exclaimed. "Yuichi, it's cold, cold, cold!" I buried my face in his arm, gripping it fiercely. His warm sweater smelled of autumn leaves.

"Surely it'll be a little warmer in Izu," Yuichi said, almost contemplatively. I kept my face pressed to his side.

"How long did you say you're staying?" he said, not moving. His voice resonated directly into my ear.

"Four days and three nights." I gently pulled myself away.

"You should come back feeling a little bit better, and we'll go out for tea again, okay?" He looked at me, smiling.

I nodded, got out of the car, and waved good-bye.

As I watched him drive off, I thought, I can't say *everything* that happened today was unpleasant.

Whether she or I were winning or losing, who could say? Who could know which of us was in the better position? The score couldn't be determined. Besides, there was no standard of measure, and, particularly on this cold night, I couldn't even hazard a guess.

A memory of Eriko, the saddest one of all.

Of all the many plants in her terrace window, the one she had acquired first was the potted pineapple. She told me about it once.

"It was the dead of winter. I was still a man then, Mikage. A handsome man, even though my eyes were different and my nose was a little flatter. Because I hadn't had the plastic surgery yet, you see? Even I can't remember what I looked like anymore."

It was a summer dawn and the air was chilly. Yuichi was away for the night, and Eriko had brought back a customer's gift of meat buns. As was my habit, I was taking notes while watching a cooking program I had recorded the day before. The blue dawn sky was slowly beginning to grow lighter in the east.

"Shall we eat these meat buns? It was so sweet of him to bring them to me," she had said, turning on the broiler and making jasmine tea. Suddenly she launched into the story.

I was a little surprised. I had assumed she was going to relate some unpleasant incident at the club. I listened sleepily. Her voice sounded like a voice in a dream.

"It was a long time ago, you see. Yuichi's mother was dying. I was a man, and she was my wife. She had cancer. At this point it was getting worse by the day. Anyhow, because we loved each other so much, every day I went to be with her at the hospital. I foisted Yuichi on a neighbor. I had a job then, so I sat with her before and after work, every spare minute. Yuichi would come with me on Sundays, but he was too young to know what was going on. I had what you could call a desperate faith; I still had hope, no matter how little. Each day for me was the darkest in the world. I didn't feel it so much at the time, but she was in an even darker place."

Eriko cast down her eyes, as if she were telling the sweetest of stories. In the blue light she looked thrillingly beautiful.

"My wife said one day, 'How I'd love to have some living thing in this room. . . .' Living things were connected to the sun; I thought, a plant, yes, a plant. She urged me to get a big potted plant, one that didn't require much care. I raced to the flower shop, overjoyed that there was something I could give her. A typical male, at that time I didn't know benjamin from saintpaulia. I only knew I didn't want a cactus, so I bought her a pineapple plant. It was a plant I could understand; it had little fruit growing on it and everything. When I carried it into the sickroom she looked delighted and thanked me again and again.

"She was getting closer and closer to the end. One evening, three days before she went into a coma, she said to me, just as I was leaving, 'Please take the pineapple home.' To look at her she didn't seem worse than usual. Naturally we hadn't told her she had cancer, but it was as if she knew, as if she were whispering her last wishes. I was surprised and said, 'Why? I can see that it's withering, but wouldn't you rather have it?' But she begged me, in tears, to take it home, this sunny plant from a southern place, before it became infused with death. I had no choice. I took it in my arms.

"Because I was crying my eyes out, I couldn't take a taxi. It was colder than hell, too. That may have been the first time it occurred to me I didn't like being a man. When I calmed down somewhat, after walking as far as the station and having a drink in a little bar, I took the train. That night the freezing wind whistled through the apartment. With no one there, it could hardly have been called a home. I trembled, holding the pineapple tight against my chest. The sharp leaves stuck my cheeks. In this world, tonight, only the pineapple and I understand each other— that thought came straight from my heart. Closing my eyes, as if against the cold wind, I felt we were the only two living things sharing that loneliness. My wife, who understood me better than anyone, was by now—more than I, more than the pineapple—on intimate terms with death.

"Soon after that she died, and the pineapple withered, too. I didn't know how to care for plants and had overwatered it, you see. I stuck it out in a corner of the yard, and although I couldn't have put it into words, I came to understand something. If I try to say what it is now, it's very simple: I realized that the world did not exist for my benefit. It followed that the ratio of pleasant and unpleasant things around me would not change. It wasn't up to me. It was clear that the best thing to do was to adopt a sort of muddled cheerfulness. So I became a woman, and here I am."

I understood what she was trying to say, and I remember

thinking, listlessly, is this what it means to be happy? But now I feel it in my gut. Why is it we have so little choice? We live like the lowliest worms. Always defeated—defeated we make dinner, we eat, we sleep. Everyone we love is dying. Still, to cease living is unacceptable.

Tonight, again, I felt the darkness hindering my breathing. In my heavy, depressed sleep, I battled each demon in turn.

The next day was bright and sunny, and in the morning, as I was doing some laundry for the trip, the phone rang.

It's eleven-thirty, I thought. Strange time for a phone call. Puzzled, I answered it.

"*Aaaah!*" screamed a high, thin voice. "Mikage, dear? How have you been?"

"Chika!" I exclaimed. Although she seemed to be calling from a phone booth—there were loud traffic noises in the background—I had no trouble identifying the voice. It summoned up her image in my mind.

Chika was the head girl at Eriko's club. She was, of course, a transvestite, and she often used to spend the night at the apartment. Eriko had willed the club to her.

Compared with Eriko, Chika was undeniably a man in appearance. But she (so to speak) did look rather beautiful when made up and was tall and slender. The showy dresses she wore suited her, and her manner was very gentle. One time, a little kid in the subway, making fun of her, lifted her skirt to take a look. She couldn't stop crying. She was very sensitive. Much as I hate to admit it, around her I always felt like the masculine one.

"I'm by the train station right now," she said. "Can you get away? I have to talk to you about something. Have you had lunch?"

"Not yet."

"Well then, come to Sarashina, the *soba* shop, immediately!" Ever impetuous, with that she hung up. I felt I had no choice; I stopped doing my laundry and went out.

I hurried through the neighborhood streets under the brilliant, shadowless light of high noon. I found the place among the row of shops in front of the station and went in. There was Chika, eating *soba* noodles with fried bits of tempura batter and wearing what is practically the national costume, a two-piece warmup suit.

"Chika!" I walked over to her.

"*Aaaah!*" she screamed. "It's been so long! You've grown so beautiful, I can hardly look at you—wait, let me get my sunglasses." Her warmth banished any embarrassment I might have been feeling. I only saw her untroubled smile that said to the world, "What have I got to be ashamed of?" In the presence of her brilliant face, a little bit of Chika rubbed off on me, and I ordered loudly, "Extra-thick noodles with chicken, please." The waitress, bustling about in the noon rush, slammed a glass of water down before me.

"What did you want to talk to me about?" I got to the point, slurping my noodles.

Whenever Chika "had to tell me something," it never

amounted to anything, and I expected this time to be the same. But she whispered, gravely, "It's about Yuichi."

My heart leaped with an audible thump.

"Last night he came into the club saying he couldn't sleep. He was feeling terrible. 'Let's go have some fun,' he said. Don't get me wrong, honey, I've known that boy since he was so-oo high. There's nothing funny between us, we're like parent and child. Parent and child, you know?"

I smiled. "I know, Chika."

She continued. "I was surprised. I'm crazy myself and many times I don't understand other people's feelings, but . . . That boy has never, ever, let anybody see a weakness in him before, you know that. He was on the verge of tears, and that's not like him. He kept insisting, 'Let's go somewhere.' The poor dear looked so unhappy, I was afraid he might just waste away. I really wanted to be with him, but we're right in the middle of getting the club back to normal. Everybody's still pretty jumpy around there, and I couldn't leave. I told him I couldn't, so he said dejectedly, 'I'll go somewhere by myself then.' I gave him the name of an inn I know."

"I see," I said. "I see."

"I told him, just teasing, 'Why don't you take Mikage?' I didn't mean anything by it. He answered me, dead serious, 'Aw, she's going to Izu for her job. Besides, I don't want to get her mixed up in my problems. Now that she's doing so well and all, it wouldn't be right to drag her down.' Then it hit me—they're in love. Of course, no doubt about it, you're in love. I'm going to give you the address and phone number of the inn. Mikage, why don't you go after him?"

"Chika," I said, "I have to go on a trip for work tomorrow." I was in shock.

I felt I understood Yuichi's feelings as if I held them in my own two hands. Like me, but a hundred times more so, he had to get far away somewhere. He wanted to be alone, someplace where he wouldn't have to think about anything. To escape from it all, including me. Maybe he was even thinking of not coming back for some time. I was sure of it.

"What's this about work?" Chika leaned toward me. "In a time like this, there's only one thing for a woman to do. What's the matter, honey, still a virgin? Or, oo-ooh, I get it. You two haven't slept together yet?"

"Chika!" I exclaimed, appalled. Still, a part of me thought, wouldn't it be a better world if everyone were like Chika? In her eyes I saw reflected a far happier picture of Yuichi and me than was in fact the case.

"I'll think about it," I said. "I just heard about Eriko and I'm still all confused, but it must be much worse for Yuichi. I have to be very gentle with him."

Chika looked up from her noodles, her face serious. "I know," she said. "You see, I wasn't working that night and I didn't witness dear Eriko's death. So in a way I still haven't accepted it. But I knew the man. He came to the club all the time. If Eriko had only confided in me, I'm sure it could have been prevented. Yuichi is the same way. It's such a shame. One night we were watching the news together, and that gentle boy suddenly said, with a frightening look on his face, 'People who kill people should all be dead.' Yuichi is all alone in the world now. Eriko always handled her own problems no matter what they were. He got that from her, and this is the dark side of that independence. It's gone too far!"

One by one the tears slipped down Chika's face. When she began to sob audibly, "*Wah. Wah.*" everyone in the place turned to stare at her. Chika's shoulders jerked spasmodically, racked with grief. Tears fell into her soup.

"Mikage dear, I'm so miserable. Why do things like this have to happen? I can't believe in the gods. We'll never see dear Eriko again, and I can't bear it."

I walked Chika, who was still sobbing, from the restaurant to the station, my arm around her tall shoulders.

"I'm so sorry," she said, dabbing at her eyes with a lace handkerchief. At the turnstile she slipped me a note with the directions to Yuichi's inn and the phone number. She may be just a bar girl, I thought, but her knowledge of the right spots to press was impeccable.

Deeply moved, I watched her broad back disappear.

It was true that she jumped to conclusions and that her life was a mess—even her earlier stint as a salesman had been a failure. I was aware of all that, but the beauty of her tears was something I would not soon forget. She made me realize that the human heart is something very precious.

Under the blue sky, inhaling the clear, sharp bite of winter air, I was overwhelmed by it all. What should I do? I had no idea. The sky was blue, blue. The bare trees were sharply silhouetted, and a cold wind was seeping through.

"I can't believe in the gods."

* * *

The next day I set out for Izu as planned.

With our small group—*Sensei*, several staff members, and a cameraman—it promised to be a pleasant trip. The daily schedule was not demanding. Yes, I thought, this is a dream trip. A gift from above. I felt I was being set free from the events of the last half-year.

That last half-year . . . Until Eriko's death my relationship with Yuichi had been laughing and carefree, but under the surface it had been growing more and more complicated. The times of great happiness and great sorrow were too intense; it was impossible to reconcile them with the routine of daily life. With great effort we each tried to find a peaceful space for ourselves. But Eriko had been the dazzling sun that lit the place.

The experiences of the last months had changed me. In the mirror I could see only a trace of the spoiled princess I had been, the one who took Eriko for granted. I was so far from that now.

Staring out the window of the van at the clear, sunny landscape, I realized how terribly far I had come. I, too, was dead tired. I, too, wanted to get away from Yuichi, to find some peace. Sad, but that's how it was.

That evening I went to *Sensei*'s room in my bathrobe.

"*Sensei*," I said, "I'm dying of hunger. Do you mind if I go out and get something to eat?"

One of the older staff members, who was sharing a room with her, burst out laughing and said to me, "Poor Mikage, you didn't eat a thing at dinner, did you?" The two of them were sitting on their futons, dressed for bed.

I was starving. This inn was famous for a vegetarian cuisine consisting entirely of smelly vegetables I hate—I, who shouldn't be a picky eater—so I'd barely touched a thing. *Sensei* smiled and said it was fine with her.

It was past ten. I went back down the long corridor to my room, got dressed, and left the inn. For fear of getting locked out, I quietly unbolted the rear emergency door.

The food at this inn had been hideous, but the next day we were planning to get in the van and move on. As I walked along in the moonlight, I wished that I might spend the rest of my life traveling from place to place. If I had a family to go home to perhaps I might have felt adventurous, but as it was I would be horribly lonely. Still, it just might be the life for me. When you're traveling, every night the air is clear and crisp, the mind serene. In any case, if nobody was waiting for me anywhere, yes, this serene life would be the thing. But I'm not free, I realized; I've been touched by Yuichi's soul. How much easier it would be to stay away forever.

I walked for a while along a street thick with inns.

The dark shadows of the mountains loomed blacker than the night sky over the town below. Drunken tourists were everywhere (looking cold in their padded winter kimonos), laughing loudly. I felt strangely lighthearted. I was excited. Alone under the stars, in a strange place.

I walked along, stepping on my shadow, watching it lengthen and shorten with every streetlight I passed. Avoiding the noisy bars that frightened me, I kept going until I was almost at the station. I peered into the darkened windows of souvenir shops and I spotted the light coming from a small eatery that was still open. Through the frosted-glass door I saw it had only one customer, who was sitting at the counter. I opened the door with a sense of relief and went in.

I craved something heavy and filling, so I ordered deep-fried pork in broth over rice. "*Katsudon*, please," I said.

"I have to fry the pork," said the counterman. "It'll take a while. That okay with you?" I nodded. The place was new and smelled of clean, white wood. Everything was carefully tended; it had a good atmosphere. This sort of place usually has great food. While I waited, I spied a pink telephone an arm's length away.

I reached for it and picked up the receiver. It felt very natural to pull out Chika's note and dial the number of the inn where Yuichi was staying.

While the lady at the desk was transferring the call to Yuichi's room, I had a sudden thought. The forlornness I had felt in relation to Yuichi since hearing about Eriko's death was linked with the idea of "telephone." Since then, even when he was standing next to me, I had felt as if Yuichi were in some other world, at the other end of a telephone line. And that other world was darker than the place where I was. It was like the bottom of the sea.

Yuichi answered. "Hello?"

"Yuichi?" It was a relief to hear his voice.

"Mikage, is that you? How did you know where I was? Ah, of course, Chika." His words sounded far away, traveling over the cable, through the night. I closed my eyes, just listening to that voice I missed so much. It was like lonely waves against the shore.

"So," I said, "what do they have there, where you're staying?"

"Well, there's a Denny's. Ha, ha, just kidding. Let's see, there's a shrine on the mountaintop; I guess it's famous. At the base of the mountain there's this inn that serves nothing but tofu—what they call 'monk's food'—which is what I had for dinner."

"What kind of food is that? Sounds interesting."

"Oh, right, taking a professional interest, are you? Well, it's tofu, tofu, and more tofu. I mean, it's good, but still, it's just tofu. Savory custard, tofu baked with miso, fried tofu, citron, sesame seeds—everything with tofu. Even the clear soup is served with—surprise—egg tofu floating in it. I was dying to sink my teeth into something solid, and I thought, well, they'll have to serve rice at the end, anyway—but no! They gave us soupy rice in tea. I felt like an old man."

"That's funny—me too. I'm starving right now."

"What, don't they serve food at your inn?"

"Yes, but only things I hate."

"Tough break, huh? The odds against that are enormous."

"It's okay, though. Tomorrow we'll have great food."

"Lucky you. Let me try to guess what I'll get for breakfast . . . tofu in hot water, I'll bet."

"Right. Probably over a charcoal fire, in a little earthenware pot. Yes, that's it."

"Now that I think about it, Chika loves tofu. No wonder she said this place was so great. And it is—I mean, it has these big windows, with a view of a waterfall and all. But a growing boy like me wants nice, fattening foods, as greasy as possible. It's strange, isn't it? Both of us under the same night sky, both with empty bellies." Yuichi laughed.

I know this is incredibly stupid, but I couldn't bring myself to tell him, "Hey, I'm about to eat pork and rice!" It seemed like the worst kind of treachery. I couldn't destroy Yuichi's picture of us starving together.

At that moment I had a thrillingly sharp intuition. I knew it as if I held it in my hands: In the gloom of death that surrounded the two of us, we were just at the point of approaching and negotiating a gentle curve. If we bypassed it, we would split off into different directions. In that case we would forever remain just friends.

I knew it. I knew it with absolute certainty.

I was at a loss as to what to do. And after all it would be okay to ask.

"When are you coming back?"

After a silence Yuichi said, "Very soon."

He's a bad liar: I was sure he would stay there as long as his money held out. This was the same Yuichi who had delayed telling me about Eriko's death and kept his depression to himself. That was his nature.

"Well, see you later, then," I said.

"Right. Later." Perhaps not even he himself understood why he had to run away.

"Don't slit your wrists, okay?" I said, joking.

He laughed and said good-bye.

As soon as I hung up I was hit by a wave of exhaustion.

My hand still resting on the receiver, I stared intently at the glass door of the restaurant, listening to the wind rattling outside. People walked past, complaining about the cold. Day had turned to night, and night was passing in the same way all over the world. Now I felt really alone, at the bottom of a deep loneliness that no one could touch.

People aren't overcome by situations or outside forces; defeat invades from within, I thought. I had lost my last ounce of strength. Before my eyes something was coming to an end, something I didn't want to end, but for which I lacked the energy to suffer, much less fight. There was only a leaden hopelessness in me.

Maybe someday I'd be able to think it over calmly, in a brighter place than this, full of sunlight and flowers. But by then it would be too late.

My *katsudon* was ready. I perked up and split my chopsticks. Thinking, an army travels on its stomach, I contemplated my meal. Although it *looked* exceptionally delicious, that was nothing to the way it tasted. It was outrageously good.

"This is incredible!" I blurted out spontaneously to the counterman.

"I thought you'd like it." He smiled triumphantly.

You may say it's because I was starving, but remember, this is my profession. This *katsudon*, encountered almost by accident, was made with unusual skill, I must say. Good quality meat, excellent broth, the eggs and onions handled beautifully, the rice with just the right degree of firmness to hold up in the broth—it was flawless. Then I remembered having heard *Sensei* mention this place: "It's a pity we won't have time for it," she had said. What luck! And then I thought, ah, if only Yuichi were here. I impulsively said to the counterman, "Can this be made to go? Would you make me another one, please?"

That's how I came to find myself standing alone in the street, close to midnight, belly pleasantly full, a hot takeout container of *katsudon* in my hands, completely bewildered as to how to proceed.

Whatever was I thinking of? Now what do I do? I was wondering that when a taxi approached and squealed to a stop, which solved the dilemma. I announced my destination. "I'd like to go to Isehara, please."

"Isehara?" screeched the driver, turning to look at me. "It's more than all right with me, but it's far. It's going to be expensive, you know."

"Yes, but it's rather urgent." I acknowledged the fact calmly, like Joan of Arc before the Dauphin. I was even convincing myself it was normal. "When we get there I'll pay the fare. But I'd like you to wait about twenty minutes while I take care of some business, and then bring me back here."

"A matter of love, is it?"

I smiled ruefully. "Something along those lines."

"Okay, then, let's get going."

The taxi set off for Isehara in the night, the *katsudon* and myself in tow.

I drowsed, overcome once more by the exhaustions of the day, while we flew up the practically empty road.

Suddenly I awoke. I had a clear impression that only my consciousness was awake, while my arms and legs still slept, all nice and warm. When I sat up to look out the window in the darkened cab, the rest of my body came to life. The driver said, "We're almost there. We made good time."

I agreed and looked up at the sky.

The moon shone down from high above, crossing the sky, erasing the stars in its path. It was full. I watched it go behind a cloud, completely hidden, and reemerge. In the hot car, I fogged the window with my breath. We passed by the silhouettes of trees and fields and mountains, like cutout pictures. Once in a while a truck would roar past us, then all would go back to utter stillness. The asphalt glistened in the moonlight.

Soon we were in Isehara.

Immersed in the deep, dark night were rows of shops and houses. Mixed among the roofs of homes were the *torii* gates of numberless little Shinto shrines. We chugged up the narrow sloping road. The line of the mountain cable car swung heavily in the gloom.

The driver said, "You know, there used to be many monks in this area, and they couldn't eat meat, so they invented all these different ways to eat tofu. Nowadays the inns are quite well-known for it. You should come here for lunch sometime and try it."

"I've heard." I was squinting at the paper Chika had given me, trying to read it by the light of the evenly spaced street lamps. "Ah!" I said. "Please stop at the next corner. I'll be back soon."

"Sure thing," he said, bringing the cab to a sudden halt.

* * *

It was bone-chillingly cold, and soon my hands and cheeks were frozen. I took out my gloves and put them on. I climbed the hill in the moonlight, the *katsudon* in my backpack.

I had an uneasy premonition and it didn't prove wrong. The inn where Yuichi was staying was not the old-fashioned kind, which would have been easy to get into in the middle of the night. At the front entrance the automatic glass door was securely locked, as was the emergency exit at the bottom of the outer stairs.

I walked back down the path to call the inn, but no one answered. That was reasonable. It was midnight, after all.

I felt puzzled as I stood before the darkened building: What on earth am I doing all the way out here?

Then, unwilling to give up, I walked around to the back, inching my way along a tiny path next to the emergency exit. Just as Yuichi had said, from the garden you could see the waterfall, and each room faced the garden, which was no doubt a selling point. But every window was dark. I sighed, contemplating the situation. A railing ran along the cliff, and the high, thin stream kept up a steady sound of falling water against the mossy rocks below. White flecks of cold-looking spray gleamed in the dark. The whole waterfall was illuminated here and there by amazingly bright green lights that brought the trees into almost unnatural relief. The scene reminded me of the

Jungle Cruise at Disneyland. Thinking, what a fake-looking green, I turned around and once more gazed up at the row of darkened windows.

Just then, somehow, I knew.

The room in the near corner, the window reflecting green light—that was Yuichi's.

I felt at any moment I would be peering through that window. I began to climb up a pile of garden stones against the wall.

Looking up, I saw the edge of an ornamental ledge that ran around the building between the first and second floors. It occurred to me that I could just reach it on tiptoe. Carefully gauging the stability of the haphazardly stacked pile of stones, I took a second step, then a third, and I got even nearer. Facing a pair of shutters, I tentatively stretched out a hand. I just barely got a grip. Determined, I jumped and managed to cling fast to a shutter with one hand. Making a supreme effort, I was able to launch the other hand over the top of the ornamental ledge and held onto the tile with all my strength. Suddenly, as I hung there, pressed vertically against the side of the building, what few athletic skills I had seemed to leave me with an audible *sssshhhhh*.

Still holding fast to the tile at the jutting edge of the ornamental ledge, stretched to the maximum, I found myself in a fix. My arms were numb with cold, and my backpack was working itself off one shoulder and down my arm.

Look at you, I thought. Thanks to a sudden whim, here you are hanging from a roof, panting white puffs of breath. You've really outdone yourself this time.

The stones I had climbed up on seemed to loom dark and far away. The roaring of the waterfall reverberated desperately. I had no choice: I gave it everything I had and pulled myself up, dangling from the ledge. I lifted the top half of my body up and over, kicking off the wall with grim determination.

I heard a ripping sound, and a searing pain shot up my right arm. I managed to roll myself onto the roof on all fours. My legs made a splashing noise as I lolled in a filthy pool of what must have been rain water.

Still lying down, but having reached a haven, I looked at my arm. It was covered in red from the bleeding wound. It made me dizzy to look at it.

I shrugged off my pack. Lying there on my back, I looked up at the roof of the inn and, staring at the glowing moon and clouds, I thought, really, we're all in the same position. (It occurred to me that I had often thought that in similar situations, in moments of utter desperation. I would like to be known as an action philosopher.)

We all believe we can choose our own path from among the many alternatives. But perhaps it's more accurate to say that we make the choice unconsciously. I think I did—but now I knew it, because now I was able to put it into words. But I don't mean this in the fatalistic sense; we're constantly making choices. With the breaths we take every day, with the expression in our eyes, with the daily actions we do over and over, we decide as though by instinct. And so some of us will inevitably find ourselves rolling around in a puddle on some roof in a strange place with a takeout *katsudon* in the middle of winter, looking up at the night sky, as if it were the most natural thing in the world.

Ah, but the moon was lovely.

I stood up and knocked on Yuichi's window.

I waited for a response for what seemed like a pretty long time. The cold was beginning to penetrate through my wet pants when the light popped on in the room and Yuichi appeared, looking scared to death.

Only the upper half of my body was visible over the ledge. Yuichi stared at me, his eyes perfect circles. "Mikage?" His lips formed my name. I knocked again and nodded, yes. Flustered, he opened the window. I stretched out a frozen hand and he pulled me in.

I blinked, my eyes unaccustomed to the sudden light. The room was so warm it was like another world. In bits and pieces, my scattered mind and body seemed to become one again.

"I came to deliver a *katsudon*," I said. "It didn't seem fair that only I should get to eat, the *katsudon* was so delicious."

I took it from my backpack.

The fluorescent light shone on the new green *tatami* mat. The television was on, the sound low. The covers on the futon from which Yuichi had just risen still bore the shape of his body.

"Something like this happened to us before," said Yuichi. "Our dream conversation. Isn't this like that?"

I laughed. "Shall we sing the song? The two of us, together?" The moment I saw Yuichi I lost all sense of reality. Suddenly all the time we'd spent together, even the fact that we'd lived in the same place, seemed like a far-off dream. Yuichi was not in this world now. His cold eyes frightened me.

"Yuichi, could you make some tea? But then I have to get going again." Even if this is a dream, I wanted to add.

"Sure," he said, picking up the thermos of hot water and the teapot. He made tea. I drank it, holding the cup in both hands. Relief at last. I was coming back to life.

Then I became aware of the heavy atmosphere in the room. I felt that I was inside Yuichi's nightmare, and that if I stayed here too long I, too, would become a part of it, destined to be snuffed out in the gloom. I didn't know if it was either a hazy intuition or fate. I said, "Yuichi, you don't really want to go back, do you? You're trying to separate yourself from the strange life you've been living, you're trying to start over. It's no good lying to me. I know it." Although my words were spoken in utter desperation, I was strangely calm. "But right now there's this *katsudon*. Go ahead, eat it."

In the ensuing silence, I felt my chest compress so tightly that it made me want to cry. With downcast eyes, Yuichi guiltily took the *katsudon*. But in that tomblike atmosphere we got a boost from something I could not have foreseen.

"Mikage, what happened to your hand?" said Yuichi, noticing my wound.

I smiled and showed him my palm. "Oh, it's nothing. Come on, eat at least a little of that before it gets cold."

Although he still looked as if he didn't understand what was happening, he said, "Yes, this looks great." He removed the lid and began to eat the *katsudon* the counterman had packaged so carefully. My spirits began to lift; I had done all I could.

I knew it: the glittering crystal of all the good times we'd had, which had been sleeping in the depths of memory, was awakening and would keep us going. Like a blast of fresh wind, the richly perfumed breath of those days returned to my soul.

More family memories.

Yuichi and I playing computer games one night while we waited for Eriko to come home. After that, sleepy-eyed, the three of us going out for egg and vegetable pancakes. A hilarious comic book Yuichi had given me to keep me from dying of boredom at work. Eriko, reading it, laughing till she cried. The smell of omelets one sunny Sunday morning. The feeling of a blanket being gently pulled over me while I slept on the floor. The swish of Eriko's skirt as she walked—me barely awake, following her slender legs through half-open eyes. Yuichi bringing a drunken Eriko home in the car, the two of them walking up to the door, their arms around each other. The day of a summer festival, Eriko tightening my *obi* with a jerk; the color of a red dragonfly dancing in a frenzy in the evening air that night.

Truly happy memories always live on, shining. Over time, one by one, they come back to life. The meals we ate together, numberless afternoons and evenings.

When was it that Yuichi said to me, "Why is it that everything I eat when I'm with you is so delicious?"

I laughed. "Could it be that you're satisfying hunger and lust at the same time?"

"No way, no way, no way!" he said, laughing. "It must be because we're family."

Even in the absence of Eriko, a lighthearted mood had been reestablished between us. Yuichi eating his *katsudon*, me drinking my tea, the darkness no longer harboring death. And so it was all right again.

I stood up. "Well, I'll be going back now."

"Back?" Yuichi looked surprised. "Where to? Where did you come from?"

"You're right," I teased, wrinkling my nose. "If I tell you, this night will become reality." But I couldn't stop myself. "I came here from Izu in a taxi. You see, Yuichi, how much I don't want to lose you. We've been very lonely, but we had it easy. Because death is so heavy—we, too young to know about it, couldn't handle it. After this you and I may end up seeing nothing but suffering, difficulty, and ugliness, but if only you'll agree to it, I want for us to go on to more difficult places, happier places, whatever comes, together. I want you to make the decision after you're completely better, so take your time thinking about it. In the meantime, though, don't disappear on me."

Yuichi put down his chopsticks and looked straight into my eyes. "This is the best *katsudon* I've ever had in my life," he said. "It's incredibly delicious."

"Yes." I smiled.

"Overall, I've been pretty cold, haven't I? It's just that I wanted you to see me when I'm feeling more manly, when I'm feeling strong."

"Will you tear a telephone book in half for me?"

"That's it. Or maybe pick up a car and throw it."

101

"Or smash a truck against a wall with your bare hands."

"Just your average tough-guy stuff." Yuichi's smiling face seemed to sparkle. I knew I had touched something inside him.

"Okay, I'll be going now. The taxi's going to abandon me." With that I headed for the door.

"Mikage."

I turned around.

"Take care of yourself."

Smiling, I waved good-bye, then unbolted the door, let myself out, and ran for the taxi.

Back at the inn, the heat in my room still on, I burrowed under the covers and fell asleep, dead to the world.

I awoke with a start to the pit-a-pat of slippers and the voices of the inn employees in the hall. The world had undergone a complete change. Outside the large, modern windows, a strong wind raged, chased by dense gray clouds heavy with snow.

The night before seemed like a dream. I stood up sleepily and turned on the lights. Dancing snowflakes scattered over the mountains, clearly visible from the window. The trees swayed and roared. The overheated room was bright white.

I crawled back under the covers, still staring at that cold-looking, powerful snowstorm outside. My cheeks burned.

Eriko was no more.

Watching that scene, I really knew it for the first time.

No matter how it turned out with Yuichi and me, no matter how long or how beautiful a life I would live, I would never see her again.

Chilled-looking people walking along the riverside, the snow beginning, faintly, to pile up on the roofs of cars, the bare trees shaking their heads left and right, dry leaves tossing in the wind. The silver of the metal window sash sparkling coldly.

Soon after, I heard *Sensei* call, "Mikage! Are you awake? It's snowing, look! It's snowing!"

"I'm coming!" I called out, standing up. I got dressed to begin another day. Over and over, we begin again.

The last day, we went to a hotel in Shimoda to sample French cuisine. They threw us a fabulous banquet that night.

Why was it that the entire group was made up of people who went to bed so early? For me, a night owl, this would not do. After they all dispersed to their rooms, I went for a walk on the beach outside the hotel.

Even wrapped in my coat and wearing two pairs of stockings, I was so cold I wanted to scream. On my way out I had bought a hot can of coffee from the vending machine, and now I was carrying it in my pocket. It was *very* hot.

I stood on a seawall and looked down at the foggy mass of white over the beach. The sea was jet black, from time to time fringed with a lacy, flickering light.

As the cold wind raged around me, the night seemed to

echo in my head. I continued down the darkened steps toward the water. The frozen sand crunched beneath my feet. I walked far up the beach, beside the ocean, sipping my coffee.

The endless sea was shrouded in darkness. I could see the shadowy forms of gigantic, rugged crags against which the waves were crashing. While watching them, I felt a strange, sweet sadness. In the biting air I told myself, there will be so much pleasure, so much suffering. With or without Yuichi.

The beacon of the faraway lighthouse revolved. It turned to me, then it turned away, forming a pathway of light on the waves.

Nodding to myself, my nose dripping, I returned to my room. I took a hot shower while I waited for the tea water to boil. As I was sitting up in bed in my warm, fresh pajamas, the phone rang. When I answered it, the person at the desk said, "You have a telephone call. Please hold."

I looked down at the garden outside the window, the dark lawn, then the white gates. Beyond that was the cold beach I had just come from, and the black, undulating sea. I could hear the waves.

"Hello." Yuichi's voiced popped up. "Tracked you down at last. It wasn't easy."

"Where are you calling from?" I asked, laughing. My heart was slowly beginning to relax.

"Tokyo," said Yuichi. I had a feeling that was the entire answer.

"Today was our last day, you know. I'm coming back tomorrow."

"Did you eat a lot of good things?"

"Yes. Sashimi, prawns, wild boar. Today was French. I think I've gained a little weight. That reminds me, I sent a package jam-packed with *wasabi* pickle, eel pies, and tea by express mail to my apartment. You can go pick it up if you like."

"Why didn't you send sashimi and prawns?"

"Because there's no way to send them!" I laughed.

Yuichi sounded happy. "Too bad—I'm picking you up at the station tomorrow, so you could have carried them with you. What time are you getting in?"

The room was warm, filling with steam from the boiling water. I launched into what time I'd be in and what platform I'd be on.

———

MOONLIGHT SHADOW

Wherever he went, Hitoshi always had a little bell with him, attached to the case he kept his bus pass in. Even though it was just a trinket, something I gave him before we were in love, it was destined to remain at his side until the last.

Although we were in separate homerooms, we met serving on the same committee for the sophomore-class field trip. Because we had completely different itineraries, the only time we had together was on the bullet train itself. On the platform after we arrived, we shook hands in a playful show of regret at having to part. I suddenly remembered that I had, in the pocket of my school uniform, a little bell that had fallen off the cat. "Here," I said, "a farewell gift," and handed it to him. "What's this?" he said, laughing, and—although it wasn't the most creative gift—took it from my palm and wrapped it carefully in his handkerchief as if it were something precious. He surprised me: it was not typical behavior for a boy that age.

As it turns out, it was love.

Whether he did it because the gift was from me or because that was how he was raised, not to treat a gift carelessly, it amazed me and made me warm to him.

There was electric charge between our hearts, and its conduit was the sound of the bell. The whole time we spent apart on that class trip, we each had the bell on our minds. Whenever he heard it ring, he would remember me and the time we had spent together; I passed the trip imagining I could hear the bell across the vast sky, imagining the person who had it in his possession. After we got back, we fell deeply in love.

For nearly four years the bell was always with us. Each and every afternoon and evening, in each and every thing we did—our first kiss, our big fights, rain and shine and snow, the first night we spent together, every smile and every tear, listening to music and watching TV—whenever Hitoshi took out that case, which he used as a wallet, we heard its faint, clear tinkling sound. It seemed as though I could hear it even when he wasn't there. You might say it was just a young girl's sentimentality. But I did think I heard it—that's how it felt to me then.

There was one thing that always disturbed me profoundly. Sometimes, no matter how intently I would be staring at him, I would have the feeling that Hitoshi wasn't there. So many times, when he was asleep, I felt the need to put my ear to his heart. No matter how bright his smile, I would have to strain my eyes to see him. His facial expressions, the atmosphere around him, always had a kind of transparency. The whole time I was with him there was that feeling of ephemerality, uncertainty. If that was a premonition of what was to come, what a sorrowful one it was.

A lover should die after a long lifetime. I lost Hitoshi at the age of twenty, and I suffered from it so much that I felt as if my own life had stopped. The night he died, my soul went away to some other place and I couldn't bring it back. It was impossible to see the world as I had before. My brain ebbed and flowed, unstable, and I passed the days in a relentless state of dull oppression. I felt that I was fated to undergo one of those things it's better not to have to experience even once in a lifetime (abortion, prostitution, major illness).

After all, we were still young, and who knows whether it would have been our last love? We had over-come many first hurdles together. We came to know what it is to be deeply tied to someone and we learned to judge for ourselves the weight of many kinds of events—from these things, one by one, we constructed our four years.

Now that it's over, I can shout it out: *The gods are assholes!* I loved Hitoshi—I loved Hitoshi more than life itself.

* * *

For two months after Hitoshi died, every morning found me leaning over the railing of the bridge on the river, drinking hot tea. I had begun to go jogging every day at dawn, since I slept very badly, and that point on the bridge was where I rested before the run back home.

Sleeping at night was what I feared most. No—worse than that was the shock of awakening. I dreaded the deep gloom that would fall when I remembered he was gone. My dreams were always about Hitoshi. After my painful, fitful sleep, whether or not I had been able to see him, on awakening I would know it had been only a dream—in reality I would never be with him again. And so I tried not to wake up. Going back to sleep was no answer: depressed to the point of nausea, I would toss around in a cold sweat. Through my curtains I would see the sky getting lighter, blue-white, and I would feel abandoned in the chill and silence of dawn. It was so forlorn and cold, I wished I could be back in the dream. There I would be, wide-eyed, tortured by its lingering memory. It was always then that I truly woke up. Finally, exhausted from lack of sleep, beginning to panic at the prospect of that lonely time—like a bout of insanity—in which I would wait for the first morning light, I decided to take up running.

I bought myself an expensive two-piece sweatsuit, running shoes, and even a small aluminum container in which to carry a hot drink. I thought, ironically, that beginners always over-equip—but still, it was best to look ahead.

I began running just before spring vacation. I would run

to the bridge, turn around, and head home, where I would carefully wash out my neck towel and sweaty clothes. While they were in the dryer I would help my mother make breakfast. Then I'd go back to bed for a while. That was my life. In the evenings I'd get together with friends, watch videos, whatever, anything to leave myself as little free time as possible. But the struggle was fruitless. There was only one thing I had any desire to do: I wanted to see Hitoshi. Yet at all costs I had to keep my hands and body and mind moving. Doing that, I hoped, albeit listlessly, would somehow, someday, lead to a breakthrough. There was no guarantee, but I would try to endure, no matter what, until it came. When my dog died, when my bird died, I had gotten through in more or less the same way. But it was different this time. Without a prospect in sight, day after day went by, like losing one's mind bit by bit. I would repeat to myself, like a prayer: It's all right, it's all right, the day will come when you'll pull out of this.

The river, spanned by a white bridge, was wide, and divided our part of the city almost exactly in half. It took me about twenty minutes to reach it. I loved that place—it was there that I used to meet Hitoshi, who had lived on the other side of the river. Even after he died I still loved the place.

On the deserted bridge, with the city misted over by the blue haze of dawn, my eyes absently followed the white embankment that continued on to who knows where. I rested, enveloped in the sound of the current, leisurely drinking hot tea. Standing there in the clear air that tingled with cold, I felt just the tiniest bit close to death myself. It was only in the severe clarity of that horribly lonely place that I could feel at ease. My self-torture stopped when I was there. Without this respite I would never have been able to get through the days. I was pierced by how much I needed it.

That morning I awoke with a start from a vicious nightmare. It was five-thirty. In the dawn of what promised to be a clear day I dressed and went out as usual. It was still dark; not a soul was out. The air was bitingly cold, the streets misty white, the sky a deep navy blue. Rich gradations of red were coming up in the east.

I had to force myself to run. My breath was labored; the notion that running this much on not enough sleep was only tormenting my body passed through my mind, but I ignored it: I can sleep when I get home, I thought in my befuddled brain. The streets were so utterly quiet that I struggled to remain fully conscious.

The sound of the current grew louder as I approached the river; the colors in the sky were changing moment by moment. I was leaning over the railing the way I always did upon reaching the bridge, absently looking at the rows of buildings on the street, which hung in a faint mist, as if submerged in an ocean of blue air. The river was roaring, sweeping along anything and everything in its way on a stream of white foam. The wind it gave off blew cold and seemed to suck the perspiration from my face. A half-moon shone serenely in the still-brisk March sky. My breath came out in puffs of white. I took the cap off my aluminum bottle and poured out some tea, still looking out over the river.

Just then I suddenly heard a voice from behind me pipe up, "What kind of tea is that? Could I have some?" It startled me—so much so that I dropped the bottle in the river. I still had a full cup of steaming tea in one hand.

Imagining god knows what, I turned around, and there stood a young woman with a smile on her face. I knew she was older than me, but for some reason I couldn't guess her age. Maybe about twenty-five . . . She had short hair and very clear, large eyes. She wore a thin white coat, but seemed not to feel the cold in the least. She had popped up before I had a clue that anyone was there behind me.

Then, looking cheerful, she said in a slightly nasal but sweet voice, "It's just like that Brothers Grimm story about the dog, isn't it? Or was that Aesop?" She laughed.

"In that instance," I said coolly, "the dog dropped his bone when he saw his own reflection in the water. Nobody sneaked up behind him."

She said, smiling, "I'd like to buy you a new thermos."

"Thank you," I said, showing her a smile in return. She spoke so calmly that I was not afraid of her, and she wasn't attempting familiarities. She didn't seem crazy, nor did she look like a drunk on her way home at dawn. Her eyes were too knowing and serene; the expression on her face hinted that she had tasted deeply of the sorrows and joys of this world. The air around her seemed somehow charged.

After taking one sip to wet my throat, I offered her the

BANANA YOSHIMOTO

cup. "Here, have the rest. It's Pu–Arh tea."

"Oh, I love that," she said, taking the cup with a slender hand. "I just got here. I came from pretty far away." She looked down at the river. Her eyes had the bright sparkle of a traveler's.

"Sightseeing?" I asked, wondering what could have brought her to this particular place.

"Yes. Soon, on this spot, there'll be something to see that only happens every hundred years. Have you ever heard about it?"

"Something to see?"

"Yes. If all the conditions are right."

"What, exactly?"

"I can't tell you yet. But I promise I will, because you shared your tea with me." She laughed as she said it, and I almost failed to catch that last part. The mood of approaching morning seemed to fill the whole world. The rays of the rising sun spread over the blue sky, illuminating the faintly sparkling layers of air with white light.

It was time to be getting back, so I said, "Well, good-bye." At that she looked me directly in the eye with that same bright expression. "My name is Urara," she said. "What's yours?"

"Satsuki," I answered.

"Let's get together again," said Urara, waving good-bye.

I waved back and started running home. She was an odd one. I had no idea what she was talking about, but somehow I knew that she was someone who did not live like other people. With each step I took I grew more uneasy, and I couldn't help but turn and look back. Urara was still on the bridge. I saw her face in profile as she watched the river. It shocked me—it was not that of the person I had just talked with. I had never seen such a severe expression on anyone.

She noticed me standing there, smiled brightly again, and waved. Flustered, I returned her wave and broke into a run.

In heaven's name, what kind of person was she? I pondered it for quite some time. More and more, that morning in the sunlight, the impression of that mysterious Urara carved itself with baroque filigree into my sleepy brain.

Hitoshi had an extremely eccentric younger brother. His way of thinking, his responses to events, were "curioser and curioser." He lived exactly as if his awareness of things had been formed in some other dimension, after which he was plopped down on this planet to fend for himself. That was my first impression of him, and I stick by it. His name was Hiiragi. He was to turn eighteen this month.

Hiiragi and I had arranged to meet, after he got out of school, in a coffee shop on the fourth floor of a department store. In he came, wearing a sailor-style girl's high school uniform, complete with middy blouse and skirt.

The truth is I was mortified, but he acted so natural that

117

I managed to feign calmness. Sitting down across from me, he asked, breathless, "Were you waiting long?" When I shook my head he smiled brightly. After he had ordered, the waitress stared him up and down and muttered, "Yes, sir," mystified.

He didn't look much like Hitoshi, but sometimes the way his face and fingers moved would remind me so much of his brother that my heart would stop.

"Oh!" I said, purposely giving voice to my surprise, as I always did when he reminded me of Hitoshi. It was part of a ritual between us.

"What is it?" he said, looking at me, cup in hand.

"You . . . you reminded me of him, just then," I said. Then, according to our ritual, he said, "I'll do Hitoshi," and imitated his brother. We both laughed. That was the only way the two of us had to make light of the wounds in our hearts.

I'd lost my boyfriend, but he had lost both brother and girlfriend at once.

His girlfriend, Yumiko, had been a small, pretty girl his own age, and a tennis ace. The four of us were close in age, got along well, and had often hung out together. I would go over to Hitoshi's house and Yumiko would be there with Hiiragi—I couldn't count how many times the four of us stayed up all night, playing games.

The night it happened, Hitoshi was giving Yumiko a ride from his house, where she'd been visiting Hiiragi, to the train station. On the way they got into an accident. It wasn't his fault. Still, the two of them were killed instantly.

★   ★   ★

"So, you're jogging?" said Hiiragi.

"Yes."

"Then why are you getting so fat?"

"It must be because I lie around all afternoon," I said, laughing. The truth was, I was getting noticeably thinner.

"Sports aren't good for you—it's true," he said. "But I have an idea—they just opened this place near my house that makes incredible tempura on rice. Very fattening. Let's go there now—right now!"

Although Hitoshi and Hiiragi had been very different from each other, they were both just naturally kind in a way that was without affectation or ulterior motives. That's how they were raised. The sort of kindness that makes a person wrap a bell in a handkerchief.

"I'd love to," I said.

The girl's school uniform Hiiragi was wearing had been Yumiko's.

After she died he had started wearing it to school, though he went to one where uniforms were not required. Yumiko had liked to wear the uniform. Both sets of parents had begged him, in tears, not to do it, saying Yumiko wouldn't have liked to see him in a skirt. Hiiragi just laughed and ignored them. When I asked him if he wore it for sentimental reasons, he said that wasn't it. "Things are just things, they can't bring back the dead. It just makes me feel better."

"Are you going to wear it forever?" I asked him.

His face darkened a little. "I don't know."

"Aren't people talking about you? Aren't they saying things about you at school?"

"No, they know that's just how I am. Actually, I'm getting a lot of sympathy. And the girls are crazy about me. It must be because, wearing a skirt, perhaps they think I understand them."

I laughed. "Well, that's good, isn't it?" Outside the glass wall of the coffee shop, crowds of boisterous shoppers came and went. The whole department store that evening was jovial, and gaily illuminated spring clothes were on display.

Now I understood. His sailor outfit—my jogging. They served exactly the same purpose. I wasn't as eccentric as him, so I was satisfied with mere jogging. Because nothing so conventional would do for Hiiragi, he chose the sailor outfit, as a variation. Neither recourse was anything more than a way of trying to lend some life to a shriveled spirit. It was a way to divert our minds, to kill time.

Both Hiiragi and I, in the last two months, had unconsciously assumed facial expressions we had never worn before, expressions that showed how we were battling not to think of what we had lost. If, in a flash, we remembered, we would suddenly be crushed with the knowledge, the knowledge of our loss, and find ourselves standing alone in the darkness.

I got up. "If I'm going to eat dinner out, I have to call home and let them know. What about you? Is it okay for you not to eat at home?"

Hiiragi said, "Oh, yeah, right. My father's away on a business trip."

"So your mother's all alone. You should probably go home."

"It's okay. I'll just have something delivered to her. It's still early, so she won't have started cooking yet. I'll pay for it, and she'll get this surprise dinner—compliments of her son."

"That's a sweet idea," I said.

"It'll cheer her up, don't you think?" Hiiragi smiled artlessly. This young boy, usually so precociously adult, looked his age right then.

One winter day Hitoshi had said, "I have a younger brother. His name is Hiiragi." It was the first time I had heard of him. We were climbing the long stone stairway behind the school, under leaden gray skies that promised snow. His hands in his coat pockets, his breath a cloud of white, Hitoshi had said, "But in a way he's more grown up than I am."

"Grown up?" I laughed.

"How can I say it? . . . he thinks well on his feet. But still, when it comes to the family, he's strangely childlike. Yesterday my father nicked his hand a little on a piece of glass, and my brother freaked out—really, seriously freaked out. You would have thought the sky had fallen. I just now thought of it, his reaction was so out of proportion."

"How old is he?"

"I guess he's . . . what, fifteen?"

"Does he look like you? I'd like to meet him."

"Well, I warn you, he's pretty weird. So much so you'd never take him for my brother. I'm afraid if you meet him you might stop liking me. Yes, he certainly is an odd one," said Hitoshi, smiling a classic elder-brother smile.

"Well, is your little brother so strange that you're going to wait till years from now to introduce me, when you're sure of my unwavering love?"

"No, I was kidding. It'll be all right. I'm sure you'll get on fine. You're a little strange yourself, and Hiiragi likes 'good people.' "

" 'Good people?' "

"Right." Hitoshi laughed, still looking straight ahead. At times like that I always felt shy.

The stairs were steep and I hurried up, flustered. The windows of the white school building reflected the darkening dead-of-winter sky. I remember climbing step by step in my black shoes and knee socks; the swish, swish of the skirt of my school uniform.

Outside, the night was filled with the scent of spring. Hiiragi's sailor-style uniform was hidden under his coat, which was a relief to me. The light given off by the department-store windows shone white on the faces of the bustling crowd. In spite of the sweet smell of spring on the wind, it was still cold. I took my gloves from my pocket.

"The tempura place is near my house, so it's a bit of a walk," said Hiiragi.

"We'll cross the bridge, then, won't we?" I fell silent,

remembering the encounter with Urara. Every morning since then I had gone running, but I hadn't seen her again. I was absently thinking about that when Hiiragi suddenly said in a loud voice, "Oh!—don't worry, of course I'll drive you back." He had interpreted my silence as worrying about how I'd get home.

"No, no, that's no problem. It's still early," I said, confused, thinking, you . . . you reminded me of him just then, although this time I didn't say it. At that moment he was so like Hitoshi there was no need to ask Hiiragi to do him. A kindness spoken out of reflex, at once impersonal and generous, but by no means bridging the distance established between two people—it always produces in me that sense of transparency, that deeply moving emotion I was being reminded of right then. An unbearable sense of loss.

"The other day," I said as we set off, "one morning when I was jogging, I met a strange person on the bridge. I was just remembering that."

"A strange person? You mean a man?" Hiiragi smiled. "Jogging early in the morning can be dangerous."

"No, it's not that at all. It was a woman. Not an easy person to forget."

"Maybe you ought to see her again."

"Hmm."

It was true; for some reason I wanted terribly to see Urara. That expression on her face—it made my heart stop. She had been gentle and smiling with me, and then, as soon as she was alone again, she . . . if I had to describe it, I'd say the expression on her face was like that of a demon turned into a human who suddenly caught herself feeling emotions and was warning herself that she wasn't permitted to. It was unforgettable. I felt that my own pain and sadness had never even come close to hers. Perhaps there was still much worse in store for me.

We came to a large intersection. Both Hiiragi and I felt a little ill at ease; this was the scene of the accident. Even now cars were coming and going furiously. At the red light Hiiragi and I stopped side by side.

"I wonder if there mightn't be ghosts here." Hiiragi smiled, but his eyes weren't smiling at all.

"I thought you were going to say that," I said, trying to smile back.

The traffic signal changed, and the river of light formed by the cars continued on its way. The signal shone brightly, suspended in the darkness. Hitoshi had died here. A feeling of solemnity slowly came over me. In places where a loved one has died, time stops for eternity. If I stand on the very spot, one says to oneself, like a prayer, might I feel the pain he felt? They say that on a visit to an old castle or whatever, the history of the place, the presence of people who walked there many years ago, can be felt in the body. Before, when I heard things like that, I would think, what are they talking about? But I felt I understood it now.

This intersection, the colors of these buildings, and rows of shops in the darkness were Hitoshi's last sights. And it wasn't all that long ago.

How afraid was he? Did he think of me, if even for a

flickering instant? Was the moon climbing high in the sky as it was now?

"It's green." I was staring so absentmindedly at the moon that Hiiragi had to give me a push on the shoulder. The small white light it gave off was so pretty, so cold; it was like a pearl.

"It's amazing how good this is," I said. The tempura on rice we were eating, seated at the counter in this new little shop smelling of fresh wood, was so good it revived my appetite.

"Isn't it?" said Hiiragi.

"Yes. It's delicious. So delicious it makes me grateful I'm alive," I said. So delicious I was moved to praise extravagant enough to make the counter person blush.

"I know. I knew you'd say that. You have excellent taste in food. It really makes me happy that you like it." After saying that all in one breath, with a big smile, Hiiragi went to order the meal for his mother and have it delivered.

With the bowl of food before me, I thought: I'm stubborn, and I'll probably be dragged even deeper into this darkness, but I have no choice. I must keep living this way. But, as soon as possible, I wanted this boy to be always smiling, like he was now, like he always used to, and without the sailor outfit.

It was noon. Suddenly the phone rang.

I had caught cold and was drowsing in bed. I hadn't even

been able to go jogging. The ring of the telephone jabbed into my slightly feverish brain again and again. Sleepily I got out of bed. No one seemed to be home, so I had no choice—I went out into the hall and picked up the receiver.

"Yes?"

"Hello. Is Satsuki there?" It was an unfamiliar woman's voice.

"This is she," I said, puzzled.

"It's me," said the person across the phone lines. "Urara."

I was startled. Again she had shocked me. How in the world had she found me?

"Sorry this is so sudden, but I wonder if you're free just now? Can you come out and meet me?"

"Umm . . . sure. But why? How did you get my phone number?" I said, faltering. She seemed to be calling from a phone booth, judging by the sound of traffic in the background. I heard little puffs of laughter.

"I just say to myself, 'I *must* get this phone number,' and it just naturally comes to me," Urara said, as if reciting a spell. She said it in such a matter-of-fact, reasonable way that I thought, oh, I see.

"Meet me on the fifth floor of the department store across from the station, in the section where they sell thermoses." With that she hung up.

Normally there would be no way I'd go out now—the way I feel with this cold, I should stay in bed, I thought after she had hung up. My legs were wobbly and it felt like my fever was getting worse. But still, driven by curiosity to see her again, I started to get ready. In the innermost recess of my heart the light of instinct was twinkling, and I was as free of doubt as if I had heard the command, "Go!"

In retrospect I realize that fate was a ladder on which, at the time, I could not afford to miss a single rung. To skip out on even one scene would have meant never making it to the top, although it would have been by far the easier choice. What motivated me was probably that little light still left in my half-dead heart, glittering in the darkness. Yet without it, perhaps, I might have slept better.

I bundled up in warm clothing and got on my bike. It was a noon enveloped in warm sunlight—it made you think that spring would truly come. A light wind was blowing, soft and gentle on the face. The trees on the street were beginning to sprout their tiny infant leaves. A thin veil of mist hung distantly in the pale blue sky far beyond the city.

Such blossoming delectability did not make my own insides flutter; it left me unmoved. The spring scenery could not enter my heart for love or money. It was merely reflected on the surface, like on a soap bubble. Everyone out on the streets was coming and going, looking happy, the light shining through their hair. Everything was breathing, increasingly sparkling, swathed in the gentle sunlight. The pretty scene was brimming with life, but my soul was pining for the desolate streets of winter and for that river at dawn. I wished my heart would break and get it over with.

There stood Urara, her back to the display of water

bottles. Wearing a pink sweater, standing ramrod-straight in the midst of the crowd, this time she looked my age.

"Hi," I called. When I came nearer her eyes widened. "What?" she said. "You have a cold? Oh, I'm sorry. I didn't know when I asked you to come out."

I smiled. "Is it that obvious?"

"Yes, your face is bright red. So . . . let's choose quickly, shall we? Any one you like." She turned to face the display. "So what do you think? Probably a thermos, right? Or for running you might want a lighter one. This one is just like the one you dropped the other day. Or, oh, if it's design you care most about, let's go to where they sell ones made in China."

Her enthusiasm as she said all this made me so happy, even I could feel myself turning bright red.

"Okay, that little white one." Beaming with pleasure, I pointed out a small thermos.

"Mmm. The honored customer is a person of fine discernment," Urara said, and bought it for me.

As we were drinking barley tea in a nearby rooftop garden tea shop, Urara said, "I brought you this, too." She took a small packet from her coat pocket. Then another, and another, again and again. I could only stare.

"Somebody who owns a tea shop gave me this as a parting gift. There are all sorts of herbal teas, barley teas, Chinese teas, too. The names are written on the packages. Something to fill your thermos with. I hope you like them."

". . . Thank you, so much," I said, hesitant, pleased.

"Not at all. It was my fault you dropped yours in the river."

The afternoon was clear and bright. The light illuminating the streets was so vivid it almost made one's heart ache. Clouds moved slowly, dividing the city below into patches of light and shadow. It was a peaceful afternoon. The weather was so tranquil that it almost made me forget I had any problems at all—aside from the fact that my nose was stuffed up and I could taste only a hint of what I was drinking.

"By the way," I said, "how *did* you get my phone number, really?"

She smiled. "I told you. That was the truth. For a long time I've been on my own, moving around from place to place, and I developed this ability to just . . . sense things, calmly, like a wild animal. I don't remember exactly when that started, but . . . So I thought to myself, Satsuki's phone number is . . . ? And when I dialed, I just let my fingers move naturally. I usually get it right."

"Usually?" I smiled.

"Yes, usually. When I'm wrong I just apologize, laugh, and hang up. Still it makes me ashamed of myself." Urara laughed cheerfully.

I wanted to believe she got the number that way rather than by other, more normal methods. That's the effect she had on a person. Somewhere deep in my heart I felt I had known her long ago, and the reunion made me so nostalgic I wanted to weep tears of joy.

"I want to thank you for today. You've made me as happy as a lover," I said.

"All right, then, here's a word from your lover: get over that cold by the day after tomorrow."

"Why? Oh, is it the day after tomorrow? The something to see?"

"Precisely. All right? You mustn't tell anyone else." Urara lowered her voice a little. "The day after tomorrow, come to the place where we met the other day by no later than four fifty-seven A.M. If all goes well you may see something."

"What is this something? What kind of thing? Something invisible?" I couldn't hold back a flood of doubts.

"Yes. But it depends on the weather, and also on you. Because this is a very subtle matter, there are no guarantees. Still, and this is just my intuition, I think there's a profound connection between you and that river. That's why I'm sure you'll be able to see it. The day after tomorrow, at the time I said, in that place, if a number of conditions are met, you *may* be able to see a kind of . . . vision, something that happens only once every hundred years or so. I'm afraid 'may' is the best I can do."

That explanation didn't really clarify much, either. Still, I was deeply thrilled, something I had not felt in a long time.

"Is it a good thing?"

"Yes . . . Not just good, though—priceless. That's up to you."

That's up to me.

Just now, when I'm so weak, with no strength to defend myself . . .

"Yes," I said. "I'll be there."

*　*　*

The connection between me and the river. Even with my heart beating wildly, my mind shouted out an impromptu *yes!* The border between my country and Hitoshi's—that's what the river was to me. When I thought of the bridge, it was always with Hitoshi standing there, waiting for me to come. I was always late; he was always there before me. When we said good-bye, it was there that we parted, he going to one side of the river, me to the other. The last time was that way, too.

"So," I had said, "you're going over to Takahashi's house after this?" I was still happy then and had a healthy plumpness that I've lost now. This was our last conversation.

"Yes, after I stop off at home first. We haven't gotten all the guys together in a long time."

"Give them my regards. But I know what you all talk about when it's just guys."

"Anything wrong with that?" He laughed.

We had done nothing but have fun that whole day and, a little tipsy, we walked along laughing and joking. The bitingly cold night road was splendidly colored by the starry sky overhead, and I was lighthearted. The wind stung my cheeks, the stars twinkled. Our hands, joined in my pocket, palms touching, felt very warm and soft.

Then, "Oh," he said, as if suddenly remembering something. "But I swear, I'd never say anything bad about you!" He was so touchingly funny as he said it that I had to bury my face in my muffler to stifle my laughter. To have loved each other this much for over four years, I thought, isn't it marvelous. That me seems ten years younger than I feel now. The faint sound of the river reached our ears; the moment of our parting was approaching.

The bridge. That bridge was where we left each other, never to meet again. The river roared, and the cold wind was like a slap in the face. Amid its vivid thundering, under the sky full of stars, we exchanged a short kiss, and thinking how much fun that winter vacation had been, we parted, smiling. The tinkle of the bell disappeared into the night. Hitoshi and I both cherished that sound.

We had horrible fights and we both had our little outside flings. We suffered from the changing balance between love and desire. Children that we were, we hurt each other many times over. So it isn't that we were always as happy as we were that day; our times together were often painful. Still, it was a good four years, and that day was an unusually perfect one for us, so much so as to make us fearful it would end. Of that day in which everything was just too beautiful in the transparent winter air, what I remember most is the sight, when I turned back to look, of Hitoshi's black jacket melting into the darkness.

That scene is one I cried about over and over again. Or rather, whenever I recalled it, the tears would flow. I would dream of myself crossing the bridge, chasing after him and calling out, "You mustn't go!" In the dream, Hitoshi would smile and say, "I didn't die after all, because you stopped me."

Sometimes the memory would come to me in the middle of the day, and I would manage not to break down in public—but what good did it do me? I felt he had gone somewhere endlessly far from me, and my stoicism only made the feeling worse.

When I parted with Urara, that "something" I *might* be able to see at the river was, for me, half joke, half hope. Urara, beaming, disappeared up the street.

Maybe she's just telling me some weird kind of lie, I thought, but I wouldn't even mind if, bright and early, I ran there, chest pounding, only to make a fool of myself. She had shown my heart a rainbow. The thing was . . . she had reminded me that I could get excited over something unknown, and a tiny window opened in my heart. Even if nothing happened—even if it turned out to be just the two of us watching the sparkling glints off the cold, flowing river—it would feel good. It would be enough for me.

That was what I was thinking as I walked along, holding my thermos. On the way to get my bike where I'd left it at the station, I spotted Hiiragi.

There he was, in the middle of the street, wearing his regular clothes. He must be skipping school, I thought, which made me smile.

It wasn't that I was hesitant to run up to him and call his name—it was just that because of my fever I couldn't muster the energy, so all I did was walk toward him without changing my pace. Just then he set off in the direction I was going anyway, so quite naturally I followed him up the street. He was a fast walker, and I, unwilling to go faster, soon fell behind.

I watched Hiiragi. In his own clothes, he was good-looking enough to turn people's heads. Wearing a black sweater, he was walking along like he always did—tall, long-limbed, calm, cool, and light on his feet. No wonder, I thought as I watched him from behind, the girls couldn't get enough of him. Yumiko had died, and he was wearing her uniform in her memory. It just didn't happen that often, losing one's brother and girlfriend at once. It was the epitome of unusual. Maybe I, too, were I a carefree high school girl, would long to be the one to restore him to life and would fall in love with him. Girls that age find nothing more attractive.

If I just called out his name he would turn and smile at me. I knew that. But still, somehow I had a bad feeling about calling to him as he walked alone up the street; I felt there was nothing anyone could do for him. Or maybe it was just that I was terribly tired. Nothing could enter directly into my heart. All I wanted was to get through this as quickly as possible, to see the day when memories would be just memories. But the more I wanted that, the further away it seemed. Thinking of the future only made me shudder.

Then Hiiragi suddenly stopped, and I automatically stopped, too. Now you really are trailing him, I said to myself, smiling. I took a step toward him and was about to call out—then I realized what he was looking at and froze in my tracks.

He was staring into the window of a tennis shop. How well I understood the blank look on his face as he peered into that window. He seemed to be feeling nothing at all. But in that very lack of expression, the profundity of what he was doing was transmitted nonetheless. It's like unconscious conditioning, I thought, like a baby duck trailing after some moving object, taking it for its mother.' Though the baby duck is unaware of it, it's very touching for the observer.

That's how I felt, watching Hiiragi.

In the spring light he stood among the crowd, staring, staring detachedly into that window. The sight of all that tennis equipment must have had a powerful effect on him. It did the same thing for Hiiragi that being with him did for me: thanks to the trace of Hitoshi in him, his very presence calmed me. I thought how sad that was.

I myself saw one of Yumiko's tennis matches. The first time I met her I thought she was cute, all right, but she struck me as a bit average, rather overly cheerful, not too deep, and I couldn't imagine what Hiiragi saw in her that bewitched him so. With Yumiko, Hiiragi was in a dream. On the surface he was the same old Hiiragi, but something in her quieted his spirit. In real strength, she was his match.

"What is it about her?" I asked Hitoshi one time.

"Apparently it's tennis," he said, smiling.

"Tennis?"

"Yes. According to Hiiragi, she's incredible."

It was summer. The sun beat down mercilessly on the high school tennis court. Hitoshi, Hiiragi, and I had gone to watch Yumiko play in the finals. The shadows were deep and dark under the blazing sun; our throats were dry. Everything was dazzlingly bright.

And no doubt about it, she was incredible. She was a different person, not the little girl who ran after me laughing, calling, "Satsuki, Satsuki." I was amazed when I saw her play. Hitoshi seemed surprised, too. Hiiragi said with pride, "See what I mean? Incredible, isn't she?"

She played a take-no-prisoners game of tennis, propelled by the full force of her intensity and powers of concentration. Then I knew how strong she really was. Her face was all determination. It was a face capable of murder. Still, after the deciding shot, the instant she'd won, she turned to Hiiragi with her old baby-faced smile. It was impressive.

The four of us had a lot of fun together, and I liked her very much. She'd say to me, "Satsuki, let's the four of us always hang out together, don't you two ever break up." Teasing, I would smile and say, "Well, it won't be us." She would laugh and say, "Well, it won't be us either!"

And then it happened. It's too horrible.

I doubted if he was recalling her at this moment like I was. Boys don't go out of their way to feel pain. But still, his eyes, his whole person, were saying one thing only. He himself would never speak it. To say it would mean to suffer from it. To suffer terribly. That thing was, "I want her to come back."

More than words, it was a prayer. I couldn't bear it. Was that, then, how I looked by the river at dawn? And is that why Urara had spoken to me? Me, too. I, too, wanted to see him. I wanted him. Hitoshi. To come back. At the very least, I wanted to say a proper good-bye.

I knew I wouldn't tell Hiiragi what I'd seen today. I resolved to speak up cheerfully the next time, but for now I left without calling to him.

With all that activity, my fever went up. It makes sense, I thought; it simply follows that if one goes running around town in the condition I was in, delirious, this would be the result.

My mother laughed and asked me if it might not be like a teething fever. Weakly, I laughed back. But in a sense I think it was. Perhaps my unproductive thoughts had spread like poison throughout my body.

That night, as usual, I awoke from a dream of Hitoshi. I dreamed that in spite of my fever I had run to the river and Hitoshi was there. He said to me, smiling, "You've got a cold; what are you doing?" That was the lowest point yet. When I opened my eyes it was dawn, time to get up and get dressed. But it was cold, so very cold, and in spite of the fact that my whole body felt flushed, my hands and feet were like ice. I had the chills; I shuddered, my whole body in pain.

I opened my eyes, trembling in the half-darkness. I felt

I was battling something absurdly enormous. Then, from deep within, I began to wonder if I mightn't lose.

It hurt to have lost Hitoshi. It hurt too much.

When we were in each other's arms, I knew something that was beyond words. It was the mystery of being close to someone who is not family. My heart dropped out, and I was feeling what people fear the most; I touched the deepest despair a person can know. I was lonely. Hideously lonely. This was the worst. If I could get through this, morning would come, and I knew without a doubt that I would have fun again, laugh out loud. If only the sun would rise. If only morning would come.

Whenever it had been like this before, I had set my teeth and stood up to it; but now, lacking the strength to go to the river, I could only suffer. Time inched along, as if I were walking on shards of glass. I felt that if I could only get to the river, Hitoshi really would be there. I felt insane. I was sick at heart.

I sluggishly got up and went to the kitchen for some tea. My throat was parched. Because of my fever, the whole house looked surreally warped, distorted; the kitchen was ice-cold and dark. Everyone was asleep. Delirious, I made tea and went back to my room.

The tea seemed to help. It soothed my dry throat and my breathing became natural again. I sat up in bed and parted the curtains.

From my room I had a good view of the front gate and yard. The trees and flowers rustled, trembling in the blue morning air—they seemed painted in flat colors, like a diorama in a museum. It was pretty. These days I was well aware of how the blue air of dawn makes everything seem purified. As I sat there peering out the window, I saw the shadow of a person coming up the sidewalk in front of my house.

I wondered if it was a dream and blinked my eyes. It was Urara. Dressed in blue, grinning broadly, she looked at me and came toward me. At the gate she mouthed, "May I come in?" I nodded. She crossed the yard and reached my window. I opened it, my heart pounding.

"Sure is cold out," she said. An icy wind came in through the window, freezing my feverish cheeks. The pure, clean air tasted delicious.

"What's up?" I asked. I must have been beaming like a happy little kid.

"I'm on my way home. Your cold is looking worse, you know. Here, I'll give you some vitamin C candy." Taking the candy from her pocket, she handed it to me, smiling artlessly.

"You're always so good to me," I said in a hoarse voice.

"You look like your temperature is very high. You must feel rotten."

"Yes," I said. "I couldn't go running this morning." For some reason I felt like crying.

"With a cold"—she spoke evenly, lowering her eyes a little—"now is the hardest time. Maybe even harder than dying. But this is probably as bad as it can get. You might come to fear the next time you get a cold; it will be as bad as this, but if you just hold steady, it won't be. For the rest of your life. That's how it works. You could take the negative view and live in fear: Will it happen again? But it

won't hurt so much if you just accept it as a part of life."
With that she looked up at me, smiling.

I remained silent, my eyes wide. Was she only talking
about having a cold? Just what was she saying? The blue of
the dawn, my fever, everything was spinning, and the
boundary between dream and waking blurred. While her
words were making their way into my heart, I was staring
absently at her bangs, which were fluttering in the wind.

"Well, see you tomorrow." With a smile, Urara gently
shut the window from the outside. She skipped lightly out
the gate.

Floating in a dream, I watched her walk away. That she
had come to me at the end of a long night of misery made
me want to cry tears of joy. I wanted to tell her: "How
happy I am that you came to me like an apparition in that
bluish mist. Now everything around me will be a little bit
better when I wake up." At last I was able to fall asleep.

When I awoke I knew that my cold was at least a little
better. I slept so soundly that it was evening before I woke
up. I got out of bed, took a shower, put on a fresh change
of clothes, started drying my hair. My fever was down and
I felt quite well, except for the sensation of my body having
been through the mill.

I wondered, under the hot wind of the hair dryer, if
Urara had really come to see me. Maybe it was just a
dream—her words resounded in my brain as if it had been.
And had she really only been talking about having a cold?

My face in the mirror had a touch of dark shadow on it,

making me wonder—was this a harbinger of other terrible nights to come, like the aftershocks following an earthquake? I was so tired that I couldn't bear to think about it. I was truly exhausted. But still . . . more than anything, I wanted to evade those thoughts, even if I had to do it on my hands and knees.

For one thing, I was breathing more easily than I had been even yesterday. I was sick to death at the prospect of more suffocatingly lonely nights. The idea that they would be repeated, that that was just how life was, made me shudder with horror. Still, having tasted for myself that moment when I suddenly could breathe easy again made my heart beat faster.

I found I was able to smile a little. The knowledge of how quickly my fever had dissipated made me a little giddy. Just then there was an unexpected knock at my bedroom door. I thought it was my mother and said, "Come in." When the door opened, I was amazed to see Hiiragi.

"Your mother says she kept calling you, but you didn't answer," he said.

"I was drying my hair, I guess I couldn't hear." I was embarrassed to be caught in the intimacy of my room with just-washed, unstyled hair, but he said, nonplussed, "When I phoned, your mother said you had a cold, like a terrible teething fever, so I thought I'd come and see how you're doing."

I remembered that he'd been here with Hitoshi, like the day of the festival and that time after the baseball game. So, just like old times, he grabbed a cushion and flopped down.

141

It was only I who had forgotten how well we knew each other.

"I brought you a get-well present." Hiiragi laughed, indicating a large paper bag. At this point I couldn't tell him I was actually just about over it. I even forced a cough. He had come all this way because he thought I was sick. "It's a chicken filet sandwich from Kentucky Fried, which I know you love, and some sherbet. Cokes, too. And, I brought enough for myself, so let's eat."

He was treating me like I was made of brittle glass. My mother must have said something to him. I was embarrassed. Still, it wasn't as if I were so much better I could say flat out, "I'm completely well!"

In the brightly lit room, warmed by my little heater, the two of us calmly ate what he had brought. The food was delicious, and I realized how very, very hungry I was. It occurred to me I always enjoyed what I ate when I was with him. How wonderful that is, I thought.

"Satsuki."

"What?" In a reverie, realizing he had said my name, I looked up.

"You've got to stop torturing yourself, all alone, getting thinner and thinner—you even got a fever from it. When you feel like that, call me up. We'll get together, go do something. Every time I see you you look more frail, but you pretend everything's all right. That's a waste of energy. I know you and Hitoshi were so happy together that now you could die of sadness. It's only natural."

He had never said anything like that. It was odd—that was the first time I had seen him express such emotion:

sympathy as open and unguarded as a child's. Because I had thought his style too cool for that, it was totally unexpected, this purehearted concern. But then I remembered Hitoshi saying how Hiiragi, usually old beyond his years, reverted to a childlike state where the family was concerned. I had to smile—I felt I understood now what Hitoshi had meant.

"I know I'm still a kid, and when I take off the sailor outfit I feel so alone I could cry, but we're all brothers and sisters when we're in trouble, aren't we? I care about you so much, I just want to crawl into the same bed with you."

He said it with such an utterly sincere face, and it was so obvious his intentions were honorable, I had to smile in spite of myself. Then I said to him, deeply moved, "I'll do as you say. I really will, I'll call you, I mean it. Thank you. Really, truly, thank you."

After Hiiragi left I went back to sleep. Thanks to the cold medicine I took, I slept through a long, peaceful, dreamless night. It was the divine, anticipatory sleep I remember having slept as a child on Christmas Eve. When I awoke, I would go to Urara waiting at the river, and I would see the "something."

It was before dawn. Although my health was not quite back to normal, I got dressed and went running. It was the kind of frozen morning in which moon shadows seem to be pasted on the sky. The sound of my footsteps resonated in the silent blue air and faded away into the emptiness of the streets.

★ ★ ★

Urara was standing by the bridge. When I got there her hands were in her pockets and her muffler covered her mouth, but her sparkling eyes showed she was smiling brightly. "Good morning," she said.

The last few stars in the blue porcelain sky winked, a dim white, as if about to go out. The scene was thrillingly beautiful. The river roared furiously; the air was very clear.

"So blue it feels like it could melt right into your body," said Urara, gesturing at the sky.

The faint outline of the rustling trees trembled in the wind; gently, the heavens began to move. The moon shone through the half-dark.

"It's time." Urara's voice was tense. "Ready? What's going to happen next is, the dimension we're in—time, space, all that stuff—is going to move, shift a little. You and I, although we'll be standing side by side, probably won't be able to see each other, and we won't be seeing the same things . . . across the river. Whatever you do, you mustn't say anything, and you mustn't cross the bridge. Got it?"

I nodded. "Got it."

Then we fell silent. The only sound the roaring of the river, side by side Urara and I fixed our eyes on the far bank. My heart was pounding. I realized my legs were trembling. Dawn crept up little by little. The sky changed to a light blue. The birds began to sing.

I had a feeling that I heard something faint, far away. I looked to one side and was startled—Urara wasn't there anymore. The river, myself, the sky—then, blended with the sounds of the wind and the river, I heard what I'd longed for.

A bell. There was no question, it was Hitoshi's. The sound came, faintly tinkling, from a spot where no one was standing. I closed my eyes, making sure of the sound. Then I opened them, and when I looked across the river I felt crazier than I had in the whole last two months. I just barely managed to keep from crying out.

There was Hitoshi.

Across the river, if this wasn't a dream, and I wasn't crazy, the figure facing me was Hitoshi. Separated from him by the water, my chest welling up, I focused my eyes on that form, the very image of the memory I kept in my heart.

Through the blue haze, he was looking in my direction. He had that worried expression he always had when I acted recklessly. His hands in his pockets, his eyes found mine. The years I had spent in his arms seemed both very near and very far away. We simply gazed at each other. Only the fading moon saw the too-violent current, the too-distant chasm between us. My hair, the collar of Hitoshi's dear, familiar shirt fluttered in the wind off the river as softly as in a dream.

Hitoshi, do you want to talk to me? I want to talk to you. I want to run to your side, take you in my arms, and rejoice in being together again. But, but—the tears flowed—fate has decided that you and I be so clearly divided like this, facing each other across the river, and I don't have a say in it.

My tears fell like rain; all I could do was stare at him. Hitoshi looked sadly back at me. I wished time could stop—but with the first rays of the rising sun everything slowly began to fade away. Before my eyes, Hitoshi grew faint. When I began to panic, he smiled and waved his hand. Again and again, he waved his hand. He was disappearing into the blue void. I, too, waved. Dear, much-missed Hitoshi—I tried to burn the line of his dear shoulders, his dear arms, all of him, into my brain. The faint colors of his form, even the heat of the tears running down my cheeks: I desperately struggled to memorize it all. The arching lines described by his arm remained, like an afterimage, suspended in the air. His form was slowly growing fainter, disappearing. I stared at it through my tears.

By the time I could no longer see anything at all, everything had returned to normal: morning by the river. I looked to one side; there stood Urara. Still facing straight ahead, a heartbreaking sadness in her eyes, she asked me, "Did you see it?"

"Yes," I said, wiping away my tears.

"Was it everything you had hoped?" This time she turned to face me, smiling. Relief diffused through my heart. "It was," I said, smiling back at her. The two of us stood there in the sunshine for some time, as morning came.

★　★　★

The doughnut shop had just opened. Urara, her eyes a little sleepy, said over a hot cup of coffee, "I came to this place because I, too, lost my lover to an early death. I came hoping to say a last good-bye."

"Were you able to?" I asked.

"Yes." Urara smiled a little. "It really does happen only once every hundred years or so, and then only if a number of chance factors happen to line up right. The time and the place are not definitely set. People who know about it call it 'The Weaver Festival Phenomenon.' It can only take place near a large river. Some people can't see it at all. The residual thoughts of a person who has died meet the sadness of someone left behind, and the vision is produced. This was my first experience of it, too. . . . I think you were very lucky today."

"Every hundred years . . ." My mind raced at the thought of the probabilities involved in my having been able to see it.

"When I arrived here to take a preliminary look at the site, there you were. My animal instincts told me that you had lost someone yourself. That's why I invited you." The morning sun shone through her hair. Urara, smiling, was still as a statue while she spoke.

What kind of person was she, really? Where had she come from and where would she go from here? And who had she seen across the river? I couldn't ask her.

"Parting and death are both terribly painful. But to keep

nursing the memory of a love so great you can't believe you'll ever love again is a useless drain on a woman's energies." Urara spoke through a mouthful of doughnut, as if making casual chitchat.

"So I think it's for the best that we were able to say a proper, final good-bye today." Her eyes became terribly sad.

". . . Yes," I said. "So do I." Urara's eyes narrowed gently as she sat in the sunlight.

Hitoshi waving good-bye. It was a painful sight, like a ray of light piercing my heart.

Whether it had been for the best was not something I as yet fully understood. I only knew that, right now, sitting in the strong sunlight, its lingering memory in my breast was very painful. It hurt so much I could barely breathe.

Still . . . still, looking at the smiling Urara before me, amid the smell of weak coffee, the feeling was strong within me of having been very near the "something." I heard the windows rattle in the wind. Like Hitoshi when we parted, no matter how much I could lay bare my heart, no matter how much I strained my eyes, that "something" would remain transitory. That was certain. That "something" shone in the gloom with the strength of the sun itself; at a great speed, I was coming through. In a downpour of blessings, I prayed, as though it were a hymn: Let me become stronger.

"Where will you go now?" I asked as we walked out of the doughnut shop.

Smiling, she took my hand. "We'll meet again someday. I'll never forget your phone number."

With that, she melted into the wave of people crowding the morning streets. I watched her go and thought, I, too, will not forget. How very much you have given me.

"I saw something the other day," said Hiiragi.

I had gone to meet him to give him a birthday present during the lunch break at his high school, my alma mater. I had been waiting on a bench by the school grounds, watching the students come and go, when he came running up to me. He was no longer wearing the sailor outfit. He sat down next to me.

"You saw what?" I asked.

"Yumiko," he said. My heart skipped a beat. Students in white gym suits ran past us, kicking up dust.

"The morning of . . . was it the day before yesterday? . . ." he continued. "It may have been a dream. I was sort of half-asleep when suddenly the door opened and Yumiko walked in. It was all so normal I forgot she was dead and I said, 'Yumiko?' She smiled, put her finger to her lips, and said, 'Shhhhh.' She went to my closet, carefully took out the sailor outfit, and bundled it up in her arms. Then, her lips silently forming 'Bye-bye,' she waved good-bye. I didn't know what to do—I fell back asleep, thinking it must have been a dream. But the sailor outfit is gone. I looked everywhere for it. Then I just suddenly burst out crying."

"Hmm," I said. Could it be that it could happen somewhere other than the river? It was the right day, the right morning. With Urara gone I had no way of knowing for sure. But he was so calm about it. There was more to Hiiragi than met the eye. Perhaps he had the power to draw an event to himself that should only have occurred at the river.

"Do you think I've lost my mind?" he asked, jokingly.

In the faint spring afternoon sunshine, the lunch hour hubbub coming from the school building carried on the wind. I laughed, gave him his present, a record, and said, "I recommend jogging when you feel like that."

Hiiragi laughed, too. Sitting there in the light, he laughed and laughed.

Hitoshi:

I'll never be able to be here again. As the minutes slide by, I move on. The flow of time is something I cannot stop. I haven't a choice. I go.

One caravan has stopped, another starts up. There are people I have yet to meet, others I'll never see again. People who are gone before you know it, people who are just passing through. Even as we exchange hellos, they seem to grow transparent. I must keep living with the flowing river before my eyes.

I earnestly pray that a trace of my girl-child self will always be with you.

For waving good-bye, I thank you.

Afterword

For a very long time there was something I wanted to say in a novel, and I wanted, no matter what it took, to continue writing until I got the saying of it out of my system. This book is what resulted from that history of persistence.

Growth and the overcoming of obstacles are inscribed on a person's soul. If I have become any better at fighting my daily battles, be they violent or quiet, I know it is only thanks to my many friends and acquaintances. I want to dedicate this, my virgin offering, to them.

I supported myself by working as a waitress the whole time I was writing this novel. I want to express my deep gratitude, first, to the manager of the restaurant, Mr. Tokuji Kakinuma, for kindly turning a blind eye when I neglected my duties to write at work, as well as to all my fellow workers, and especially to Ms. Yumi Masuko, who designed the format of the book. Then I would like to thank Professors Hiroyoshi Sone and Masao Yamamoto of the Department of Arts of Nihon University for supporting me for the prize for "Moonlight Shadow." It made me so very happy.

I want to dedicate "Kitchen," Part 1, to Mr. Hiroshi Terada of Fukutake Shoten, my publisher; "Full Moon" (or "Kitchen," Part 2) to Mr. Akio Nemoto, also of Fukutake Shoten; and "Moonlight Shadow" to Mr. Jiro Yoshikawa, who introduced me to Mike Oldfield's wonderful piece of music of the same name, which was the inspiration for that novella. Lastly, I want to dedicate the book in its entirety to my father, who deserves credit for the happy fact of its having come out. I don't have space to detail the many other thanks I owe, but I hope you all will accept a general one. You have my heartfelt gratitude.

Finally, to all the readers who do not know me personally, who were kind enough to take the trouble to read my small effort, I know no greater happiness than that it may have cheered you, even a little. Surely we will meet someday, and until that day, I pray that you will live happily.

Banana Yoshimoto

About the Author

Banana Yoshimoto was born in 1964. Her first story, "Moonlight Shadow," won the Nihon University Department of Arts Prize in 1986; "Kitchen" won the prestigious *Kaien* magazine New Writer Prize in 1987. *Kitchen*, which was published in 1988, has sold millions of copies in Japan and is currently in its fifty-seventh printing. Banana Yoshimoto is also the author of two novels, *N.P.* and *Tugumi*, two collections of short stories, and two books of essays. She lives in Tokyo.